Childhood

TOVE DITLEVSEN

Childhood

Translated by TIINA NUNNALLY

PENGUIN BOOKS

PENGUIN CLASSICS

UK | USA | Canada | Ireland | Australia
India | New Zealand | South Africa

Penguin Books is part of the Penguin Random House group of companies
whose addresses can be found at global.penguinrandomhouse.com

First published as *Barndom* in Denmark 1967
Translation first published in the United States of America by
The Seal Press 1985
Published by Penguin Books 2019
001

Set in 11.63/14.66 pt Dante MT Std
Typeset by Jouve (UK), Milton Keynes
Printed and bound in Great Britain by Clays Ltd, Elcograf S.p.A.

ISBN: 978-0-241-39193-8

www.greenpenguin.co.uk

Penguin Random House is committed to a
sustainable future for our business, our readers
and our planet. This book is made from Forest
Stewardship Council® certified paper.

Childhood

I

In the morning there was hope. It sat like a fleeting gleam of light in my mother's smooth black hair that I never dared touch; it lay on my tongue with the sugar and the lukewarm oatmeal I was slowly eating while I looked at my mother's slender, folded hands that lay motionless on the newspaper, on top of the reports of Spanish flu and the Treaty of Versailles. My father had left for work and my brother was in school. So my mother was alone, even though I was there, and if I was absolutely still and didn't say a word, the remote calm in her inscrutable heart would last until the morning had grown old and she had to go out to do the shopping in Istedgade like ordinary housewives.

The sun broke over the gypsy wagon, as if it came from inside it, and Scabie Hans came out with bare chest and a wash basin in his hands. When he had poured the water over himself, he put out his hand for a towel and Pretty Lili gave it to him. They didn't say a word to each other; they were like pictures in a book when you quickly turn the pages. Like my mother, they would change in a few hours. Scabie Hans was a Salvation Army soldier and Pretty Lili was his sweetheart.

In the summer, they packed a bunch of little children into the green wagon and drove into the country with them. Parents paid one krone a day for this. I had gone myself when I was three years old and my brother was seven. Now I was five and the only thing I could remember from the trip was that Pretty Lili once set me out of the wagon, down in the warm sand in what I thought was a desert. Then the green wagon drove away from me and got smaller and smaller and inside of it sat my brother and I was never going to see him or my mother again. When the children came back home, they all had scabies. That's how Scabie Hans got his name. But Pretty Lili was not pretty. My mother was, though, on those strange and happy mornings when I would leave her completely in peace. Beautiful, untouchable, lonely, and full of secret thoughts I would never know. Behind her on the flowered wallpaper, the tatters pasted together by my father with brown tape, hung a picture of a woman staring out the window. On the floor behind her was a cradle with a little child. Below the picture it said, 'Woman awaiting her husband home from the sea'. Sometimes my mother would suddenly catch sight of me and follow my glance up to the picture I found so tender and sad. But my mother burst out laughing and it sounded like dozens of paper bags filled with air exploding all at once. My heart pounded with anguish and sorrow because the silence in the world was now broken, but I laughed with her because my mother expected me to, and because I was seized by the same cruel mirth as she was. She shoved the chair aside, got up and stood in front of the picture in her wrinkled nightgown, her hands on her hips. Then, with a clear and defiant little-girl voice that didn't belong to her in the same way as her voice did later in the day when she'd start haggling about prices with the shopkeepers, she sang:

Can't I sing
Whatever I wish for my Tulle?
Visselulle, visselulle, visselulle.
Go away from the window, my friend,
Come back another time.
Frost and cold have brought
The old beggar home again.

I didn't like the song, but I had to laugh loudly because my mother sang it to amuse me. It was my own fault, though, because if I hadn't looked at the picture, she wouldn't have noticed me. Then she would have stayed sitting there with calmly folded hands and harsh, beautiful eyes fixed on the no-man's-land between us. And my heart could have still whispered 'Mother' for a long time and known that in a mysterious way she heard it. I would have left her alone for a long time so that without words she would have said my name and known we were connected to each other. Then something like love would have filled the whole world, and Scabie Hans and Pretty Lili would have felt it and continued to be colored pictures in a book. As it was, right after the end of the song, they began to fight and yell and pull each other by the hair. And right away, angry voices from the stairwell began to push into the living room, and I promised myself that tomorrow I would pretend the wretched picture on the wall wasn't even there.

When hope had been crushed like that, my mother would get dressed with violent and irritated movements, as if every piece of clothing were an insult to her. I had to get dressed too, and the world was cold and dangerous and ominous because my mother's dark anger always ended in her slapping my face or pushing me against the stove. She was foreign and strange, and I thought that I had been exchanged at birth and she wasn't my mother at all. When she was dressed, she stood in front of the mirror in the bedroom, spit on a piece of pink tissue paper, and rubbed it hard across her cheeks. I carried the cups out to the kitchen, and inside of me long, mysterious words began to crawl across my soul like a protective membrane. A song, a poem, something soothing and rhythmic and immensely pensive, but never distressing or sad, as I knew the rest of my day would be distressing and sad. When these light waves of words streamed through me, I knew that my mother couldn't do anything else to me because she had stopped being important to me. My mother knew it, too, and her eyes would fill with cold hostility. She never hit me when my soul was moved in this way, but she didn't talk to me, either. From then on, until the following morning, it was only our bodies that were close to each other. And, in spite of the cramped space, they avoided even the slightest contact with each other. The sailor's wife on the wall still watched longingly for her husband, but my mother and I didn't need men or boys in our world. Our peculiar and infinitely fragile happiness thrived only when we were alone together; and when I stopped being a little child, it never really came back except in rare, occasional glimpses that have become even more dear to me now that my mother is dead and there is no one to tell her story as it really was.

2

Down in the bottom of my childhood my father stands laughing. He's big and black and old like the stove, but there is nothing about him that I'm afraid of. Everything that I know about him I'm allowed to know, and if I want to know anything else, I just have to ask. He doesn't talk to me on his own because he doesn't know what he should say to little girls. Once in a while he pats me on the head and says, 'Heh, heh.' Then my mother pinches her lips together and he quickly takes his hand away. My father has certain privileges because he's a man and provides for all of us. My mother has to accept that but she doesn't do it without protest. 'You could sit up like the rest of us, you know,' she says when he lies down on the sofa. And when he reads a book, she says, 'People turn strange from reading. Everything written in books is a lie.' On Sundays, my father drinks a beer and my mother says, 'That costs twenty-six øre. If you keep at it like this, we'll end up in Sundholm.' Even though I know Sundholm is a place where you sleep on straw and get salt herring three times a day, the name goes into the verse I make up when I'm scared or alone, because it's beautiful like the picture in one of my father's books that I'm so fond of. It's called 'Worker family on a picnic', and it shows a father and mother and their two children. They're sitting on some green grass and all of them are laughing while they eat from the picnic basket lying between them. All four of them are looking up at a flag stuck into the grass near the father's head. The flag is solid red. I always look at the picture upside down since I only get a chance to see it when my father is reading the book. Then my mother turns on the light and draws the yellow curtains even though it's not dark yet. 'My father was a scoundrel and a drunkard,' she says, 'but at least he wasn't a socialist.' My father keeps on reading calmly because he's slightly deaf, and that's no secret, either. My brother Edvin sits and pounds nails into a board and afterwards pulls them out with pliers. He's going to be a skilled worker. That's something very special. Skilled workers have real tablecloths on the table instead of newspaper and they eat with a knife and fork. They're never unemployed and they're not socialists. Edvin is handsome and I'm ugly. Edvin is smart and I'm stupid. Those are eternal truths like the printed white letters on the baker's roof down the street. It says, '*Politiken* is the best newspaper'. Once I asked my father why he read *Social-Demokraten* instead, but he just wrinkled his brow and cleared his throat while my mother and Edvin burst into their paper-laughter because I was so incredibly stupid.

The living room is an island of light and warmth for many thousands of evenings – the four of us are always there, like the paper dolls up on the wall behind the pillars in the puppet theater my father made from a model in *Familie Journalen*. It's always winter, and out in the world it's ice cold like in the bedroom and the kitchen. The living room sails through time and space, and the fire roars in the stove. Even though

Edvin makes lots of noise with his hammer, it seems like an even louder sound when my father turns a page in the forbidden book. After he has turned many pages, Edvin looks at my mother with his big brown eyes and puts the hammer down. 'Won't Mother sing something?' he says. 'All right,' says my mother, smiling at him, and at once my father puts the book down on his stomach and looks at me as if he'd like to say something to me. But what my father and I want to say to each other will never be said. Edvin jumps up and hands my mother the only book she owns and cares about. It's a book of war songs. He stands bending over her while she leafs through it, and though of course they don't touch each other, they're together in a way that excludes my father and me. As soon as my mother starts to sing, my father falls asleep with his hands folded over the forbidden book. My mother sings loudly and shrilly, as if dissociating herself from the words she sings:

> Mother – is it Mother?
> I see that you have wept.
> You have walked far, you have not slept.
> I am happy now. Don't cry, Mother.
> Thank you for coming, despite all this horror.

There are many verses to all of my mother's songs, and before she reaches the end of the first one, Edvin starts hammering again and my father is snoring loudly. Edvin has asked her to sing in order to avert her rage over my father's reading. He is a boy and boys don't care for songs that make you cry if you listen to them. My mother doesn't like me to cry, either, so I just sit there with a lump in my throat and look sideways down at the book, at the picture of the battlefield where the dying

9

soldier stretches his hand up toward the luminous spirit of his mother, who I know isn't there in reality. All of the songs in the book have a similar theme, and while my mother is singing them I can do whatever I want because she's so completely absorbed in her own world that nothing from outside can disturb her. She doesn't even hear it when they start to fight and argue downstairs. That's where Rapunzel with the long golden braid lives with her parents who haven't yet sold her to the witch for a bunch of bluebells. My brother is the prince and he doesn't know that soon he'll be blind after his fall from the tower. He pounds nails into his board and is the family's pride and joy. That's what boys are, while girls just get married and have children. They have to be supported and they can't hope for or expect anything else. Rapunzel's father and mother work at Carlsberg, and they each drink fifty beers a day. They keep on drinking in the evening after they've come home, and a little before my bedtime they start yelling and beating Rapunzel with a thick stick. She always goes to school with bruises on her face or legs. When they get tired of beating her, they attack each other with bottles and broken chair legs and the police often come to get one of them – and then quiet finally falls over the building. Neither my mother nor my father likes the police. They think Rapunzel's parents should be allowed to kill each other in peace if they want to. 'They're doing the big shots' work,' my father says about the police, and my mother has often talked about the time the police came and got her father and put him in jail. She'll never forget it. My father doesn't drink and he's never been in jail, either. My parents don't fight and things are much better for me than for them when they were children. But a dark edge of fear still invades all my thoughts when things have gotten quiet downstairs and I have to go to bed. 'Good night,' says my mother and closes the door, and goes into the warm living room again. Then I take off my dress, my woolen petticoat and bodice, and the long black stockings I get as a Christmas present every year. I pull my nightgown over my head and sit down on the windowsill for a minute. I look into the dark courtyard way down below and at the front building's wall that's always crying as if it has just rained. There are hardly ever lights in any of the windows because those are the bedrooms, and decent people don't sleep with the light on. Between the walls I can see a little square scrap of sky, where a single star sometimes shines. I call it the evening star and think about it with all my might when my mother has been in to turn off the light, and I lie in my bed watching the pile of clothes behind the door change into long crooked arms trying to twist around my throat. I try to scream, but manage only a feeble whisper, and when the scream finally comes, the whole bed and I are both sopping wet with sweat. My father stands in the doorway and the light is on. 'You just had a nightmare,' he says. 'I suffered from them a lot when I was a child, too. But those were different times.' He looks at me speculatively, and seems to be thinking that a child who has such a good life shouldn't be having nightmares. I smile at him shyly and apologetically, as if the scream were just a foolish whim. I pull the comforter all the way up to my chin because a man shouldn't see a girl in her nightgown. 'Well, well,' he says, turning off the light and leaving again, and in some way or other he takes my fear with him, for now I calmly fall asleep, and the clothes behind the door are only a pile of old rags. I sleep to escape the night that trails past the window with its train of terror and evil and danger. Over on Istedgade, which is so light and festive during the day, police cars and ambulances wail while

I lie securely hidden under the comforter. Drunken men lie in the gutter with broken, bloody heads, and if you go into Café Charles, you'll be killed. That's what my brother says, and everything he says is true.

3

I am barely six years old and soon I'll be enrolled in school, because I can read and write. My mother proudly tells this to everyone who bothers listening to her. She says, 'Poor people's children can have brains too.' So maybe she loves me after all? My relationship with her is close, painful, and shaky, and I always have to keep searching for a sign of love. Everything I do, I do to please her, to make her smile, to ward off her fury. This work is extremely exhausting because at the same time I have to hide so many things from her. Some of the things I get from eavesdropping, others I read about in my father's books, and still others my brother tells me. When my mother was in the hospital recently, we were both sent to Aunt Agnete's and Uncle Peter's. That's my mother's sister and her rich husband. They told me that my mother had a bad stomach, but Edvin just laughed and later explained to me that mother had 'ambortated'. A baby had been in her stomach, but it had died in there. So they had cut her open from her navel down and removed the baby. It was mysterious and terrible. When she came home from the hospital, the bucket under the sink was full of blood every day. Every time I think about it, I see a picture in front of me. It's in Zacharias Niel-sen's short stories and depicts a very beautiful woman in a long red dress. She's holding a slim white hand under her breast and saying to an elegantly dressed gentleman, 'I'm carrying a child under my heart.' In books, such things are beautiful and unbloody, and it reassures and comforts me. Edvin says that I'll get lots of spankings in school because I'm so odd. I'm odd because I read books, like my father, and because I don't understand how to play. Even so, I'm not afraid when, holding my mother's hand, I go in through the red doorway of Enghavevej School, because lately my mother has given me the completely new feeling of being something unique. She has on her new coat, with the fur collar up around her ears and belt around her hips. Her cheeks are red from the tissue paper, her lips too, and her eyebrows are painted so that they look like two little fish flicking their tails out toward her tem-ples. I'm convinced that none of the other children has such a beautiful mother. I myself am dressed in Edvin's made-over clothes, but no one can tell because Aunt Rosalia did it. She's a seamstress, and she loves my brother and me as if we were her own children. She doesn't have any herself.

When we enter the building, which seems completely empty, a sharp smell strikes my nose. I recognize it and my heart stiffens because it's the already well-known smell of fear. My mother notices it, too, because she releases my hand as we go up the stairs. In the principal's office, we're received by a woman who looks like a witch. Her greenish hair perches like a bird's nest on top of her head. She only has glasses for one eye, so I guess the other lens was broken. It seems to me that she has no lips – they're pressed so tightly together – and over them a big porous nose juts out, its tip glowing red. 'Hmm,' she says without introduction, 'so your name is Tove?' 'Yes,' says my mother, to whom she has hardly cast a glance, let alone offered a chair, 'and she can read and write without mistakes.' The woman gives me a look as if I were something she had found under a rock. 'That's too bad,' she says coldly. 'We have our own method for teaching that to children, you know.' The blush of shame floods my cheeks, as always when I've been the cause of my mother suffering insult. Gone is my pride, destroyed is my short-lived joy at being unique. My mother moves a little bit away from me and says faintly, 'She learned it by herself, it's not our fault.' I look up at her and understand many things at once. She is smaller than other adult women, younger than other mothers, and there's a world outside my street that she fears. And whenever we both fear it together, she will stab me in the back. As we stand there in front of the witch, I also notice that my mother's hands smell of dish soap. I despise that smell, and as we leave the school again in utter silence, my heart fills with the chaos of anger, sorrow, and compassion that my mother will always awaken in me from that moment on, throughout my life.

4

In the meantime, there exist certain facts. They are stiff and immovable, like the lampposts in the street, but at least they change in the evening when the lamplighter has touched them with his magic wand. Then they light up like big soft sunflowers in the narrow borderland between night and day, when all the people move so quietly and slowly, as if they were walking on the bottom of the green ocean. Facts never light up and they can't soften hearts like *Ditte menneskebarn*, which is one of the first books that I read. 'It's a social novel,' says my father pedantically, and that probably is a fact, but it doesn't tell me anything, and I have no use for it. 'Nonsense,' says my mother, who doesn't care for facts, either, but can more easily ignore them than I can. Whenever my father, on rare occasions, gets really mad at her, he says she's full of lies, but I know that's not so. I know every person has their own truth just as every child has their own childhood. My mother's truth is completely different from my father's truth, but it's just as obvious as the fact that he has brown eyes while hers are blue. Fortunately, things are set up so that you can keep quiet about the truths in your heart; but the cruel, gray facts are written in the school records and in the history of the world and in the law and in the church books. No one can change them and no one dares to try, either – not even the Lord, whose image I can't separate from Prime Minister Stauning's, even though my father says that I shouldn't believe in the Lord since the capitalists have always used Him against the poor.

Therefore:

I was born on December 14, 1918, in a little two-room apartment in Vesterbro in Copenhagen. We lived at Hedebygade 30A; the 'A' meant it was in the back building. In the front building, from the windows of which you could look down on the street, lived the finer people. Though the apartments were exactly the same as ours, they paid two kroner more a month in rent. It was the year that the World War ended and the eight-hour day was instituted. My brother Edvin was born when the World War began and when my father worked twelve-hour days. He was a stoker and his eyes were always bloodshot from the sparks from the furnace. He was thirty-seven years old when I was born, and my mother was ten years younger. My father was born in Nykøbing Mors. He was born out of wedlock and he never knew who his father was. When he was six years old, he was sent out as a shepherd boy, and at about the same time his mother married a potter named Floutrup. She had nine children by him, but I don't know anything about all of these half brothers and half sisters because I've never met them, and my father has never talked about them. He cut off ties with everyone in his family when he went to Copenhagen at the age of sixteen. He had a dream of writing and it never really left him completely. He managed to get hired as an apprentice reporter with some newspaper or other, but, for unknown reasons, he gave it up again. I know nothing of how he spent the ten years in Copenhagen until, at twenty-six, he met my mother in a bakery on Tordenskjoldsgade. She was sixteen, a sales-girl in the front of the shop where my father was a baker's assistant. It turned out to be an abnormally long engagement that my father broke off many times when he thought my mother was cheating on him. I think that most of the time it was completely innocent. Those two people were just so totally different, as if they each came from their own planet. My father was melancholy, serious, and unusually moralis-tic, while my mother, at least as a young girl, was lively and silly, irresponsible and vain. She worked as a maid at various places, and whenever something didn't suit her, she would just leave. Then my father had to go and get the servant's con-duct book and the chest-of-drawers, which he would drive over on a delivery bicycle to the new place, where there would be something else that didn't suit her. She herself once confided to me that she'd never been at any job long enough to have time to boil an egg.

I was seven years old when disaster struck us. My mother had just knit me a green sweater. I put it on and thought it was pretty. Toward the end of the day we went over to pick up my father from work. He worked at Riedel & Lindegaard on Kingosgade. He had always worked there – that is, for as long as I'd been alive. We got there a little too early, and I went and kicked at the mounds of melting snow along the curb while my mother stood leaning against the green railing, waiting. Then my father strode out of the gate and my heart began to beat faster. His face was gray and funny and different. My mother quickly went up to him. 'Ditlev,' she said, 'what's hap-pened?' He looked down at the ground. 'I've been fired,' he said. I didn't know the word but understood the irreparable damage. My father had lost his job. That which could only strike others, had hit us. Riedel & Lindegaard, from which everything good had come until now – even down to my Sunday five øre that I couldn't spend – had become an evil and horrible dragon that had spewed out my father from its fiery jaws, indifferent to his fate, to us, to me and my new green sweater that he didn't even notice. None of us said a word on the way home. I tried to slip my hand into my mother's, but she knocked my arm away with a violent motion. When we got into the living room my father looked at her with an expression heavy with guilt. 'Well, well,' he said, stroking his black mustache with two fingers, 'it'll be a long time before the unemployment benefits give out.' He was forty-three and too old to get a steady job anymore. Even so, I remember only one time when the union benefits ran out and welfare came under discussion. It happened in whispers and after my brother's and my bedtime, because it was an indelible shame like lice and child support. If you went on welfare, you lost your right to vote. We never starved, either, at least my stomach was always full of something, but I got to know the half-starvation you feel at the smell of dinner coming from the doors of the more well-to-do, when for days you've been living on coffee and stale pastry, which cost twenty-five øre for a whole school bag full.

I was the one who bought it. Every Sunday morning at six o'clock my mother woke me up and issued her orders while well hidden under the comforter in the marriage bed next to my father, who was still sleeping. With fingers that were already stiff from the cold before I reached the street, I grabbed my school bag and flew down the stairs that were pitch-dark at that time of day. I opened the door to the street and looked around in every direction and up at the front building's windows, because no one was supposed to see me perform this despicable task. It wasn't proper to take part in the school meals at the Carlsbergvej School, the only social-service institution that existed in Vesterbro in the 1930s. The latter, Edvin and I were not allowed to do. For that matter, it wasn't proper, either, to have a father who was unemployed, even though half of us did. So we covered up this disgrace with the craziest lies – the most common of which was that Father had fallen off a scaffold and was on sick leave. Over by the bakery on Tøndergade the line of children formed a winding snake along the street. They all had bags with them and they all jabbered on about how good the bread was at that particular bakery, especially when it was freshly baked. When it was my turn, I shoved the bag up on the counter, whispered my mission and added aloud, 'Preferably cream puffs.' My mother had expressly told me to ask for white bread. On the way home I stuffed myself with four or five sour cream puffs, wiped my mouth on my coat sleeve, and was never discovered when my mother rummaged in the depths of the bag. I was never, or rarely, punished for the crimes I committed. My mother hit me often and hard, but as a rule it was arbitrary and unjust, and during the punishment I felt something like a secret shame or a heavy sorrow that brought the tears to my eyes and increased the painful distance between us. My father never hit me. On the contrary – he was good to me. All of my childhood books were his, and on my fifth birthday he gave me a wonderful edition of *Grimms' Fairy Tales*, without which my childhood would have been gray and dreary and impoverished. Still, I didn't hold any strong feeling for him, which I often reproached myself for when, sitting on the sofa, he would look at me with his quiet, searching glance, as if he wanted to say or do something in my direction, something that he never managed to express. I was mother's girl and Edvin was father's boy – that law of nature couldn't be changed. Once I said to him, 'Lamentation – what does that mean, Father?' I had found the expression in Gorky and loved it. He considered this for a long time while he stroked the turned-up ends of his mustache. 'It's a Russian term,' he said then. 'It means pain and misery and sorrow. Gorky was a great poet.' I said happily, 'I want to be a poet too!' Immediately he frowned and said severely, 'Don't be a fool! A girl can't be a poet.' Offended and hurt, I withdrew into myself again while my mother and Edvin laughed at the crazy idea. I vowed never to reveal my dreams to anyone again, and I kept this vow throughout my childhood.

5

It's evening and I'm sitting as usual up on the cold windowsill in the bedroom and looking down at the courtyard. It's the happiest hour of my day. The first wave of fear has subsided. My father has said good night and has gone back to the warm living room, and the clothes behind the door have stopped frightening me. I look up at my evening star that's like God's benevolent eye; it follows me vigilantly and seems closer to me than during the day. Someday I'll write down all of the words that flow through me. Someday other people will read them in a book and marvel that a girl could be a poet, after all. My father and mother will be prouder of me than of Edvin, and a sharp-sighted teacher at school (one that I haven't had yet) will say, 'I saw it already when she was a child. There was something special about her!' I want so badly to write down the words, but where in the world would I hide such papers? Even my parents don't have a drawer that can be locked. I'm in the second grade and I want to write hymns because they're the most beautiful things that I know. On my first day of school we sang: 'God be thanked and praised, we slept so peacefully'; and when we got to 'now lively like the bird, briskly like the fish of the sea, the morning sun shines through the pane', I was so happy and moved that I burst out crying, at which all the children laughed in the same way as my mother and Edvin laugh whenever my 'oddness' brings forth my tears. My classmates find me unceasingly, overwhelmingly comical, and I've gotten used to the clown role and even find a sad comfort in it, because together with my confirmed stupidity, it protects me against their peculiar meanness toward anyone who is different.

A shadow creeps out from the arched doorway like a rat from its hole. In spite of the dark, I can see that it's the pervert. When he's certain that the way is clear, he pushes his hat down on his forehead and runs over to the pissoir, leaving the door ajar. I can't see in, but I know what he's doing. The time is past when I was afraid of him, but my mother still is. A little while ago, she took me to the Svendsgade Police Station and, indignant and trembling with rage, told the officer that women and children in the building weren't safe from his filthiness. 'He scared my little girl here out of her wits,' she said. Then the officer asked me whether the pervert had bared himself, and I said no with great conviction. I only knew the word from the line 'thus we bare our heads each time the flag is raised'. He had really never taken off his hat. When we got home, my mother said to my father, 'The police won't do anything. There's no law or justice left in this country.'

The door opens on its screeching hinges and the laughter and songs and curses break through the solemn silence in the room and inside of me. I crane my neck to get a better look at who's coming. It's Rapunzel, her father, and Tin Snout, one of her parents' drinking companions. The girl is walking between the two men, each with an arm around her neck. Her golden hair shines as if reflecting the glow from some invisible streetlamp. Roaring, they stagger across the courtyard, and a little later I can hear their ruckus out on the stairway. Rapunzel's real name is Gerda, and she is almost grown-up, at least thirteen years old. Last summer, when she went with Scabie Hans and Pretty Lili in the gypsy wagon to mind the smallest children, my mother said, 'I guess Gerda has got herself more than just scabies on this trip.' The big girls said something similar in the trash-can corner in the courtyard, where I often find myself on the outskirts. They said it in a low voice, giggling, and I didn't understand any more than that it was something shameless and dirty and obscene, something about Scabie Hans and Rapunzel. So I got up my courage and asked my mother what really had happened to Gerda. Angrily and impatiently she said, 'Oh, you goose! She's not innocent anymore, that's all.' And I wasn't any the wiser.

I look up at the cloudless, silken sky and open the window in order to be even closer to it. It's as if God slowly lowers His gentle face over the earth and His great heart beats softly and calmly, very close to mine. I feel very happy, and long, melancholy lines of verse pass through my soul. They separate me, unwillingly, from those I should be closest to. My parents don't like the fact that I believe in God and they don't like the language I use. On the other hand, I'm repelled by their use of language because they always employ the same vulgar, coarse words and expressions, the meanings of which never cover what they want to say. My mother starts almost all of her orders to me by saying, 'God help you, if you don't . . .' My father curses God in his Jylland dialect, which is perhaps not as bad, but not any nicer to listen to. On Christmas Eve we sing social democratic battle songs as we walk around the tree, and my heart aches with anguish and shame because we can hear the beautiful hymns being sung all around in the building, even in the most drunken and ungodly homes. You should respect your father and mother, and I tell myself that I do, but it's harder now than when I was little.

A fine, cool rain strikes my face and I close the window again. But I can still hear the soft sound of the hallway door as it's opened and closed far below. Then a lovely creature slips across the courtyard as if held upright by a delicate, transparent umbrella. It's Ketty, the beautiful, spiritlike woman from the apartment next to ours. She has on silver high-heel shoes under a long yellow silk dress. Over it she has a white fur that makes you think of Snow White. Ketty's hair is black as ebony, too. It takes only a minute before the arched doorway hides the beautiful sight that cheers my heart night after night. Ketty goes out every evening at this time, and my father says that it's scandalous when there are children around, and I don't understand what he means. My mother doesn't say anything, because during the day she and I are often over in Ketty's living room drinking coffee or hot chocolate. It's a wonderful room, where all the furniture is red plush. The lampshades are red, too, and Ketty herself is pink and white like my mother, although Ketty is younger. They laugh a lot, those two, and I laugh with them even though I seldom understand what's so funny. But whenever Ketty starts to talk to me, my mother sends me away because she doesn't approve of that. It's the same with Aunt Rosalia, who also likes to talk to me. 'Women who don't have children,' says my mother, 'are always so busy with other people's.' Afterwards she puts Ketty down because she makes her old mother live in the unheated room overlooking the courtyard and never lets her come into the living room. The mother is called Mrs Andersen; and, according to my mother, that's 'the blackest lie', since she's never been married. It's a great sin then to have a child – I know that. And when I ask my mother why Ketty treats her mother so badly, she says it's because the mother won't tell her who her father is. When you think about something that terrible, you really have to be grateful you have the proper relationships in your own family.

When Ketty has disappeared, the door to the pissoir opens cautiously, and the pervert edges sideways like a crab along the wall of the front building and out the door. I had completely forgotten about him.

6

Childhood is long and narrow like a coffin, and you can't get out of it on your own. It's there all the time and everyone can see it just as clearly as you can see Pretty Ludvig's harelip. It's the same with him as with Pretty Lili, who's so ugly you can't imagine she ever had a mother. Everything that is ugly or unfortunate is called beautiful, and no one knows why. You can't get out of childhood, and it clings to you like a bad smell. You notice it in other children – each childhood has its own smell. You don't recognize your own and sometimes you're afraid that it's worse than others'. You're standing talking to another girl whose childhood smells of coal and ashes, and suddenly she takes a step back because she has noticed the terrible stink of your childhood. On the sly, you observe the adults whose childhood lies inside them, torn and full of holes like a used and moth-eaten rug no one thinks about anymore or has any use for. You can't tell by looking at them that they've had a childhood, and you don't dare ask how they managed to make it through without their faces getting deeply scarred and marked by it. You suspect that they've used some secret shortcut and donned their adult form many years ahead of time. They did it one day when they were home alone and their childhood lay like three bands of iron around their heart, like Iron Hans in Grimms' fairy tale, whose bands broke only when his master was freed. But if you don't know such a short-cut, childhood must be endured and trudged through hour by hour, through an absolutely interminable number of years. Only death can free you from it, so you think a lot about death, and picture it as a white-robed, friendly angel who some night will kiss your eyelids so that they never will open again. I always think that when I'm grown-up my mother will finally like me the way she likes Edvin now. Because my childhood irritates her just as much as it irritates me, and we are only happy together whenever she suddenly forgets about its existence. Then she talks to me the way she talks to her friends or to Aunt Rosalia, and I'm very careful to make my answers so short that she won't suddenly remember I'm only a child. I let go of her hand and keep a slight distance between us so she won't be able to smell my childhood, either. It almost always happens when I go shopping with her on Istedgade. She tells me how much fun she had as a young girl. She went out dancing every night and was never off the dance floor. 'I had a new boyfriend every night,' she says and laughs loudly, 'but that had to stop when I met Ditlev.' That's my father and otherwise she always calls him 'Father', just as he calls her 'Mother' or 'Mutter'. I get the impression there was a time when she was happy and different, but that it all came to an abrupt end when she met Ditlev. When she talks about him it's as if he's someone other than my father, a dark spirit who crushes and destroys everything that is beautiful and light and lively. And I wish that this Ditlev had never come into her life. When she gets to his name, she usually catches sight of my childhood and looks at it angrily and threateningly, while the dark rim around her blue iris grows even darker. This childhood then shivers with fear and despairingly tries to slip away on tiptoe, but it's still far too little and can't be discarded yet for several hundred years.

People with such a visible, flagrant childhood both inside and out are called children, and you can treat them any way you like because there's nothing to fear from them. They have no weapons and no masks unless they are very cunning. I am that kind of cunning child, and my mask is stupidity, which I'm always careful not to let anyone tear away from me. I let my mouth fall open a little and make my eyes completely blank, as if they're always just staring off into the blue. Whenever it starts singing inside me, I'm especially careful not to let my mask show any holes. None of the grownups can stand the song in my heart or the garlands of words in my soul. But they know about them because bits seep out of me through a secret channel I don't recognize and therefore can't stop up. 'You're not putting on airs?' they say, suspiciously, and I assure them that it wouldn't even occur to me to put on airs. In school they ask, 'What are you thinking about? What was the last sentence I said?' But they never really see through me. Only the children in the courtyard or in the street do. 'You're going around playing dumb,' a big girl says menacingly and comes up close to me, 'but you're not dumb at all.' Then she starts to cross-examine me, and a lot of other girls gather silently around me, forming a circle I can't slip through until I've proved I really am stupid. At last it seems clear to them after all of my idiotic replies, and reluctantly they make a little hole in the circle so I can just squeeze through and escape to safety. 'Because you shouldn't pretend to be something you're not,' one of them yells after me, moralistic and admonishing.

Childhood is dark and it's always moaning like a little animal that's locked in a cellar and forgotten. It comes out of your throat like your breath in the cold, and sometimes it's too little, other times too big. It never fits exactly. It's only when it has been cast off that you can look at it calmly and talk about it like an illness you've survived. Most grownups say that they've had a happy childhood and maybe they really believe it themselves, but I don't think so. I think they've just managed to forget it. My mother didn't have a happy childhood, and it's not as hidden away in her as it is in other people. She tells me how terrible it was when her father had the D.T.'s and they all had to stand holding up the wall so that it wouldn't fall on him. When I say that I feel sorry for him, she yells, 'Sorry! It was his own fault, the drunken pig! He drank a whole bottle of schnapps every day, and in spite of everything, things were a lot better for us when he finally pulled himself together and hanged himself.' She also says, 'He murdered my five little brothers. He took them out of the cradle and crushed their heads against the wall.' Once I ask my Aunt Rosalia, who is mother's sister, whether this is true, and she says, 'Of course it's not true. They just died. Our father was an unhappy person, but your mother was only four years old when he died. She has inherited Granny's hatred of him.' Granny is their mother, and even though she's old now, I can imagine that her soul can hold a lot of hatred. Granny lives on the island of Amager. Her hair is completely white and she's always dressed in black. Just as with my father and mother, I may only address her in an indirect way, which makes all conversations very difficult and full of repetitions. She makes the sign of the cross before she cuts the bread, and whenever she clips her fingernails, she burns the clippings in the stove. I ask her why she does this, but she says that she doesn't know. It was something her mother did. Like all grownups, she doesn't like it when children ask about something, so she gives short answers. Wherever you turn, you run up against your childhood and hurt yourself because it's sharp-edged and hard, and stops only when it has torn you completely apart. It seems that everyone has their own and each is totally different. My brother's childhood is very noisy, for example, while mine is quiet and furtive and watchful. No one likes it and no one has any use for it. Suddenly it's much too tall and I can look into my mother's eyes when we both get up. 'You grow while you're asleep,' she says. Then I try to stay awake at night, but sleep overpowers me and in the morning I feel quite dizzy looking down at my feet, the distance has grown so great. 'You big cow,' the boys on the street yell after me, and if it keeps on like this, I'll have to go to Stormogulen where all the giants grow. Now childhood hurts. It's called growing pains and doesn't stop until you're twenty. That's what Edvin says, who knows everything – about the world and society, too – like my father, who takes him along to political meetings; my mother thinks it will end in both of them being arrested by the police. They don't listen when she says things like that because she knows as little about politics as I do. She also says that my father can't find work because he's a socialist and belongs to the union, and that Stauning, whose picture my father has hung up on the wall next to the sailor's wife, will lead us into trouble one day. I like Stauning, whom I've seen and heard many times in Fælled Park. I like him because his long beard waves so gaily in the wind and because he says 'comrades' to the workers even though he's Prime Minister and could allow himself to be more stuck-up. When it comes to politics, I think my mother is wrong, but no one is interested in what girls think or don't think about such things.

One day my childhood smells of blood, and I can't avoid noticing and knowing it. 'Now you can have children,' says my mother. 'It's much too soon, you're not even thirteen yet.' I know how you have children because I sleep with my parents, and in other ways you can't help knowing it, either. But even so, somehow I still don't understand, and I imagine that at any time I can wake up with a little child beside me. Her name will be Baby Maria, because it will be a girl. I don't like boys and I'm not allowed to play with them, either. Edvin is the only one I love and admire, and he's the only one I can imagine myself marrying. But you can't marry your brother and even if you could, he wouldn't have me. He's said that often enough. Everyone loves my brother, and I often think his childhood suits him better than mine suits me. He has a custom-made childhood that expands in tune with his growth, while mine is made for a completely different girl. Whenever I think such thoughts, my mask becomes even more stupid, because you can't talk to anyone about these kinds of things, and I always dream about meeting some mysterious person who will listen to me and understand me. I know from books that such people exist, but you can't find any of them on my childhood street.

7

Istedgade is my childhood street – its rhythm will always pound in my blood and its voice will always reach me and be the same as in those distant times when we swore to be true to each other. It's always warm and light, festive and exciting, and it envelops me completely, as if it were created to satisfy my personal need for self-expression. Here I walked as a child holding my mother's hand, and learned important things like an egg in Irma costs six øre, a pound of margarine forty-three øre, and a pound of horse meat fifty-eight øre. My mother haggles over everything except food, so that the shopkeepers wring their hands in despair, declaring she'll drive them to wrack and ruin if this keeps up. She's so wonderfully audacious, too, that she dares to exchange shirts that my father has worn as if they were brand new. And she can go right in the door of a store, stand at the end of the line and yell in a shrill voice, 'Hey, it's my turn now. I've certainly waited long enough.' I have fun with her and I admire her Copenhagen boldness and quick-wittedness. The unemployed hang around outside the small cafés. They whistle through their fingers at my mother, but she doesn't give them the time of day. 'They could at least stay at home,' she says, 'like your father.' But it's so depressing to see him sitting idly on the sofa whenever he's not out looking for work. In a magazine, I read this line: 'To sit and stare at two fists that our Lord has made so magnificently skilled.' It's a poem about the unemployed and it makes me think of my father.

It's only after I meet Ruth that Istedgade becomes a playground and permanent hangout for me after school until dinner time. At that time I'm nine years old and Ruth is seven. We notice each other one Sunday morning when all of the children in the building are chased out into the street to play so the parents can sleep late after the week's drudgery or dreariness. As usual, the big girls stand gossiping in the trash-can corner while the little ones play hopscotch, a game I always make a mess of because I either step on the line or touch the ground with my swinging leg. I never understand what the point is and find the game terribly boring. Somebody or other has said that I'm out, and resignedly I'm leaning against the wall. Then quick footsteps pound down the front building's kitchen stairway, which leads out into the courtyard, and a little girl emerges with red hair, green eyes, and light brown freckles across the bridge of her nose. 'Hi,' she says to me and grins from ear to ear, 'my name is Ruth.' I introduce myself shyly and awkwardly, because no one is used to new children making such a cool entrance. Everyone is staring at Ruth, who doesn't seem to notice it. 'Want to run and play?' she says to me, and after a hesitating glance up at our window I follow her, as I will follow her for many years, right up until we've both finished school and our profound differences have become apparent.

Now I've got a friend and it makes me much less dependent on my mother, who of course doesn't like Ruth. 'She's an adopted child and nothing good ever comes of that,' my mother says darkly, but she doesn't forbid me to play with her. Ruth's parents are a pair of big, ugly people who themselves could never have brought something as lovely as Ruth into the world. The father is a waiter and drinks like a fish. The mother is obese and asthmatic and hits Ruth for the slightest reason. Ruth doesn't care. She shakes off the claws, roars down the kitchen stairs, shows all of her shining white teeth in a smile, and says gaily, 'That bitch, I wish she'd go to hell.' When Ruth swears it isn't ugly or offensive because her voice is so crisp and fine, like the little Billy Goat Gruff. Her mouth is red and heart-shaped with a narrow, upturned upper lip, and her expression is as strong as that of the man who knew no fear. She is everything that I'm not, and I do everything she wants me to do. She cares as little as I do for real games. She never touches her dolls and she uses her doll buggy as a springboard when we put a plank on it. But we don't do that very often because the landlady comes running after us or we're told to stop it by our watchful mothers who have much too good a view from the windows. Only on Istedgade are we away from any supervision, and that's where my criminal path begins. Ruth accepts sweetly and good-humoredly that I'm not prepared to steal. But then I have to distract the clerk's attention from her tiny, quick figure that indiscriminately grabs things while I stand there asking when they expect to get bubblegum in the store. We go into the nearest doorway and share the plunder. Sometimes we go to stores and endlessly try on shoes or dresses. We select the most expensive one and politely say that our mother will come in to pay for it if they would kindly put the goods aside for the time being. Even before we get out the door, our delighted giggles break loose.

Throughout the whole long friendship, I'm always afraid of revealing myself to Ruth. I'm afraid that she'll discover how I really am. I make myself into her echo because I love her and because she's the strongest, but deep inside I am still me. I have my dreams about a future beyond the street, but Ruth is intimately tied to it and will never be torn away from it. I feel as if I'm deceiving her by pretending that we're of the same blood. In a mysterious way I am indebted to her; together with fear and a vague guilty feeling, this burdens my heart and colors our relationship in the same way it will color all close and lasting relationships later in my life.

The shoplifting comes to an abrupt end. One day Ruth has pulled off a coup by swiping a whole jar of orange marmalade inside her coat. Afterwards, we eat ourselves sick on it. Completely stuffed, we throw the rest into one of the garbage cans, which is so full that it can't be closed. So we jump up and sit on the lid. Suddenly Ruth says, 'Why the hell does it always have to be me?' 'The receiver is as bad as the thief,' I say, terrified. 'Yes, but still . . .' grumbles Ruth, 'you could do it once in a while.' I can see the reasonableness in her demand and promise uneasily to do it next time. But I insist it has to be very far away, so on Søndre Boulevard I pick out a dairy store that looks suitably deserted. Ruth cautiously opens the door and sails in, followed by her long shadow, which could very well be her own slumbering conscience. The shop is empty and there's no window in the door out to the back room. On the counter there's a bowl full of twenty-five-øre chocolate sticks in red and green foil. I stare at them, pale with excitement and fear. I lift my hand, but it's held back by invisible powers. I shake all the way down to my feet. 'Hurry up,' whispers Ruth, who is keeping an eye on the back room. Then the hand-that-can't-steal reaches up to the bowl, grabs some of the red and green dancing before my eyes, and knocks the whole pile over behind the counter. 'Idiot,' hisses Ruth, and races off just as the back door bangs open. A pale woman comes rushing out and stops, astonished, when she sees me standing there like a pillar of salt with a piece of chocolate in one upraised hand. 'What's the meaning of this?' she says. 'What are you doing here? Oh, look, now the bowl is broken!' And she bends down and picks up the pieces, and I don't know what to do, since the world hasn't crashed around me after all. I wish that it would happen now, right there. All I feel is a boundless, burning shame. The excitement and the adventure are gone; I'm just an ordinary thief, caught in the act. 'You could at least say you're sorry,' says the woman as she goes out with the shards of glass. 'Such a big, clumsy oaf.'

All the way down by Enghavevej, Ruth is standing laughing so hard she has tears in her eyes. 'You're such a blithering idiot,' she manages to say. 'Did she say anything? Why didn't you get out of there? Hey, do you still have the chocolate? Let's go to the park and eat it.' 'Do you really want to eat it?' I ask in disbelief. 'I think we should throw it under a tree.' 'Are you crazy?' Ruth says. 'Good chocolate?' 'But Ruth,' I say, 'we'll never do it again, will we?' Then my little friend asks me whether I'm becoming a goody-goody, and in the park she stuffs the chocolate in her mouth right before my eyes. After that the stealing expeditions stop. Ruth doesn't want to do it alone. And whenever my mother sends me out shopping, I always barge into the store with unnecessary noise. If, after that, it still takes a while for the clerk to come, I stand far away from the counter with my eyes on the ceiling. But my cheeks still flush red when the woman appears, and I have to control myself to keep from desperately turning my pockets inside out in front of her so she can see they're not full of stolen goods. The episode increases my guilt feeling toward Ruth, and also makes me afraid of losing her prized friendship. So I show even greater daring in our other forbidden games, such as trying to be the last one to run over the tracks in front of the train under the viaduct on Enghavevej. Sometimes I'm toppled over by the air pressure from the locomotive, and I lie on the grass embankment for a long time, gasping for breath. It's reward enough when Ruth says, 'Good God! That time you just about kicked the bucket!'

8

It's fall and the storm rattles the butcher's signs. The trees on Enghavevej have lost nearly all of their leaves, which almost cover the ground with their yellow and reddish-brown carpet that looks like my mother's hair when the sun plays in it, and you suddenly discover it's not totally black. The unemployed are freezing, but still standing erect with their hands deep in their pockets and a burned-out pipe between their teeth. The streetlamps have just been lit, and now and then the moon peeks out between racing, shifting clouds. I always think there is a mystical understanding between the moon and the street, like between two sisters who have grown old together and no longer need any language to communicate with each other. We're walking in the fleeting dusk, Ruth and I, and soon we'll have to leave the street, which makes us eager for something to happen before the day is over. When we reach Gasværksvej, where we usually turn around, Ruth says, 'Let's go down and look at the whores. There are probably some who have started.' A whore is a woman who does it for money, which seems to me much more understandable than to do it for free. Ruth told me about it, and since I think the word is ugly, I've found another in a book: 'Lady-of-the-evening'. It sounds much nicer and more romantic. Ruth tells me everything about those kinds of things; for her, the adults have no secrets. She has also told me about Scabie Hans and Rapunzel, and I can't comprehend it, since I think Scabie Hans is a very old man. And he has Pretty Lili, besides. I wonder whether men can love two women at once. For me the grownups' world is still just as mysterious. I always picture Istedgade as a beautiful woman who's lying on her back with her hair near Enghaveplads. At Gasværksvej, which forms the boundary between decent people and the depraved, her legs part, and sprinkled over them like freckles are the welcoming hotels and the bright, noisy taverns, where later in the night the police cars drive by to pick up their scandalously intoxicated and quarrelsome victims. That I know from Edvin, who is four years older than me, and is allowed to be out until ten o'clock at night. I admire Edvin greatly when he comes home in his blue Danish Youth shirt and talks politics with my father. Lately they're both very outraged over Sacco and Vanzetti, whose pictures stare out from the poster displays and the newspaper. They look so handsome with their dark foreign faces, and I also think it's too bad they're going to be executed for something they didn't do. But I just can't get as excited about it as my father, who yells and pounds the table whenever he discusses it with Uncle Peter. He's a Social Democrat like my father and Edvin, but he doesn't think that Sacco and Vanzetti deserve a better fate since they're anarchists. 'I don't care,' yells my father furiously and pounds the table. 'Miscarriage of justice is miscarriage of justice, even if it concerns a conservative!' I know that's the worst thing you can be. Recently, when I asked whether I could join the Ping Club because all the other girls in my class were members, my father looked at my mother sternly, as if I were a victim of her subversive influence in political matters, and said, 'There, you see, Mutter. Now she's becoming a reactionary. It will probably end with us subscribing to *Berlingske Tidende!*'

Down by the train station life is in full swing. Drunken men stagger around singing with their arms around each other's shoulders, and out of Café Charles rolls a fat man whose bald head strikes the pavement a couple of times before he lies still at our feet. Two officers come over to him and kick him emphatically in the side, which makes him get up with a pitiful howl. They pull him roughly to his feet and push him away when he once again tries to go into the den of iniquity. As they continue down the street, Ruth puts her fingers in her mouth and sends a long whistle after them, a talent I envy. Near Helgolandsgade there's a big crowd of laughing, noisy children, and when we go over there I see that it's Curly Charles, who is standing in the middle of the road, putting the steaming horse droppings in his mouth. All the while he's singing an indescribably filthy song that makes the children scream with laughter and give him shouts of encouragement in the hope he'll provide them with more entertainment. His eyes roll wildly. I find him tragic and horrifying, but pretend he amuses me because of Ruth, who laughs loudly along with the others. Of whores, however, we see only a couple of older, fat women who energetically wiggle their hips in an apparently vain attempt to attract the favors of an audience driving slowly by. This disappoints me greatly, because I thought all of them were like Ketty, whose evening errands in the city Ruth has also explained to me. On the way home, we go through Revalsgade, where once an old woman who owned a cigar store was murdered. We also stop in front of the haunted house on Matthæusgade and stare up at the fourth floor window where a little girl was murdered last year by Red Carl, a stoker my father worked with at the Ørsted Works. None of us dares go past that house alone at night. In the doorway at home, Gerda and Tin Snout are standing in such a tight embrace that you can't tell their figures apart in the dark. I hold my breath until I'm out in the courtyard because there's always a rancid stench of beer and urine. I feel oppressed as I go up the stairs. The dark side of sex yawns toward me more and more, and it's becoming harder to cover it up with the unwritten, trembling words my heart is always whispering. The door next to Gerda's opens quietly as I go by, and Mrs Poulsen signals me to come inside. According to my mother, she's 'shabby-genteel', but I know that you can't be both shabby and genteel. She has a lodger who my mother contemptuously calls 'a fine duke' even though he's a mail-man and supports Mrs Poulsen just as if they were married; they have no children, however. I know from Ruth that they live together as man and wife. Reluctantly, I obey the command and step into a living room exactly like ours except that there's a piano that is missing many keys. I sit down on the very edge of a chair and Mrs Poulsen sits on the sofa with a prying look in her pale blue eyes. 'Tell me something, Tove,' she says ingratiatingly. 'Do you know whether many gentle-men come to visit Miss Andersen?' I immediately make my eyes blank and stupid and let my jaw drop slightly. 'No,' I say, feigning astonishment, 'I don't think so.' 'But you and your mother are over there so much. Think a little. Haven't you ever seen any gentlemen in her apartment? Not even in the evenings?' 'No,' I lie, terrified. I'm afraid of this woman who wants to harm Ketty in some way. My mother has for-bidden me to visit Ketty anymore, and she only goes over there herself when my father is not around. Mrs Poulsen gets nothing else out of me and lets me go with a certain coolness. Several days later a petition goes around in the building and because of it, my parents have a fight when they come to bed and think I'm asleep. 'I'm going to sign it,' says my father, 'for the children's sake. You can at least protect them from witnessing the worst filth.' 'It's those old bitches,' says my mother hotly. 'They're jealous because she's young and pretty and happy. They can't stand me, either.' 'Stop comparing yourself to a whore,' snarls my father. 'Even though I don't have a steady job, you've never had to earn your own living – don't forget that!' It's awful to listen to, and it seems as though the fight is about something totally different, something they don't have words for. Soon the day arrives when Ketty and her mother are sitting out on the street on top of all their plush furniture, which a policeman, pacing back and forth, is guarding. Ketty looks right through all the people, full of contempt, holding her delicate umbrella up against the rain. She smiles at me, though, and says, 'Goodbye, Tove. Take care of yourself.' A little later they drive away in the moving van and I never see them again.

9

Something terrible has happened in my family. Landmands Bank has gone under and my Granny has lost all of her money. Five hundred kroner saved over an entire lifetime. It's a nasty business that only strikes the small investors. 'The rich pigs,' my father says, 'will see that they get their money.' Granny cries pitifully and dries her red eyes with a snow-white handkerchief. Everything about her is clean and neat and proper, and she always smells like the cleaners. The money was supposed to be used for her funeral, which she always seems to be thinking about. She pays money into a funeral coffer – she never can forget that I once thought this was the same as a coffin. It still makes her laugh whenever she thinks of it. I'm very fond of Granny, not at all in the same terrified way as I am of my mother. I'm allowed to visit her by myself, because that's what she wants and my mother doesn't dare go against her will. She told me Granny was very angry with her when she was expecting me because, since they'd had a boy, there was no reason to have any more children. Now Granny doesn't know how she's going to get a decent burial, since we don't have any money and Aunt

Rosalia with her drunken husband doesn't, either. Uncle Peter is certainly very rich, but with his proverbial stinginess, no one dreams of him contributing anything for his mother-in-law's funeral. Granny is seventy-three years old and she herself doesn't think she has long to live. She's even smaller than my mother, slight as a child and always dressed in black from head to toe. Her white, silky-soft hair is pinned up on her head, and she moves as nimbly as a young girl. She lives in a one-room apartment and she only has her old-age pension to live on. Whenever I visit her for coffee, I have rye bread with real butter, which I scrape back with my teeth until it's all on the last mouthful; it tastes better than anything I ever get at home. Since Edvin started his apprenticeship, he visits her every Sunday. Then she gives him a whole krone because he's the only boy in the family. My three cousins and I don't get anything. Every time I'm at Granny's, she asks me to sing in order to see whether I sing a little less off-key than last time. 'That's almost right,' she says encouragingly, even though I can hear that the tones coming from me don't sound like the ones I want to produce at all. You can't speak to her without being addressed first, but she herself likes to talk and I like to listen to her. She talks about her childhood, which was awful because she had a stepmother who practically beat her to death every other minute for the smallest trifles. Then she became a maid and was engaged to my grandfather, who was named Mundus and was a coach builder before he began to drink heavily. 'The Bellowing Drunk' they called him in the building, and when he hanged himself, Granny had to go out as a washerwoman in order to keep the wolf from the door. 'But my three little girls got a start in life,' she says with understandable pride. Once I let slip that I would have liked to have known my grandfather, and she says, 'Yes, he was handsome right up to the end, but a heartless scoundrel! If I wanted to, I could tell you things . . .' Then she presses her lips tightly together over her toothless gums and won't say any more. I think about the word 'heartless' and am afraid that I'm like my dreadful grandfather. I often have a nagging suspicion that I'm not capable of really feeling anything for anyone, with the exception of Ruth, of course. One day when I'm at Granny's and have to sing for her, I say, 'I've learned a new song in school.' And with a false and quavering voice, I sit on her bed and sing a poem I've written. It's very long and – like 'Hjalmar and Hilda', 'Jørgen and Hansigne', and all of my mother's ballads – it's about two people who can't have each other. But in my version, it ends less tragically with the following verse:

> Love, rich and young,
> bound them with a thousand chains.
> Does it matter that the bridal bed
> is found on country lanes?

When I've gotten this far, Granny wrinkles her forehead, stands up, and smooths down her dress as if defending herself from an unpleasant impression. 'That's not a nice song, Tove,' she says sternly. 'Did you really learn it in school?' I answer affirmatively, heavy-hearted because I thought she would say, 'That was very beautiful – who wrote it?' 'One must get married in a church,' says Granny mildly, 'before having anything to do with each other. But you couldn't know that, of course.' Oh, Granny! I know more than you think, but I'll keep quiet about it in the future. I think about a few years ago when I discovered with astonishment that my parents were married in February the same year that Edvin was born in April. I asked my mother how that could be possible, and she answered briskly, 'Well, you see, you never carry the first one more than two months.' Then she laughed, and Edvin and my father frowned. That's the worst thing about grownups, I think – they can never admit that just once in their lives they've acted wrongly or irresponsibly. They're so quick to judge others, but they never hold Judgement Day for themselves.

I only see the rest of my family together with my parents, or at least with my mother. Aunt Rosalia lives on Amager like Granny. I've only visited her a couple of times, because Uncle Carl, whom they call The Hollow Leg, is always sitting in the living room, drinking beer and grumbling, which isn't good for children to see. The living room is like everyone else's, with a buffet along one wall, a sofa against the other, and between them a table with four high-backed chairs. On the buffet, as in our apartment, there's a brass tray with a coffee pot, sugar bowl and cream pitcher that are never used, just polished bright and shiny for all special occasions. Aunt Rosalia sews for the department store Magasin and often visits us on her way home. Over her arm, in a big alpaca wrap, she carries the clothes that she's going to sew, and she never puts it down while she's visiting us. She's only going to stay 'a minute', and always keeps her hat on as if to deny she's been here several hours when she finally leaves. She and my mother always talk about events from their youth, and in that way I find out a lot that I shouldn't know. Once, for example, my mother hid a barber in the wardrobe in her room because my father unexpectedly came to visit. If my mother hadn't gotten him to leave again, the barber would have suffocated. There are lots of stories like that, and they laugh heartily at them all. Aunt Rosalia is only two years older than my mother, while

Aunt Agnete is eight years older and wasn't really young with them. She and Uncle Peter often come to play cards with my parents. Aunt Agnete is pious and suffers from it whenever someone swears in her presence, which her husband does frequently just to annoy her. She is tall and wide and has a Dagmar cross resting on her bosom, which Uncle Peter calls the balcony. If I were to believe my parents, he is evil and cunning incarnate, but he's always friendly to me, so I don't really believe them. He's a carpenter and never out of work. They live in a three-room apartment in Østerbro and have an ice-cold parlor with a piano, and they only set foot in it on Christmas Eve. It's said that Uncle Peter inherited an enormous sum of money that he keeps in various bank accounts in order to fool the tax authorities. Sometimes the employees at the shop where he works are invited to visit other companies, where they are hosted free-of-charge. When he went with them to Tuborg, he drank so much that he had to be taken to the hospital and have his stomach pumped out the following day. And when he visited the Enighed Dairy, he downed so much milk he was sick for the next week. Otherwise he never drinks anything but water. My three cousins are all older than me and rather ugly. Every evening they sit around the dinner table, knitting furiously. 'But they're not too bright,' says my father, and there's not so much as a single book in that whole big apartment. My parents make no bones about saying we've turned out better than those girls. Uncle Peter was married once before, and from that marriage he has a daughter who's only seven or eight years younger than my mother. Her name is Ester, and she's a great hulk with a wriggling, bent-over walk. Her eyes look like they're about to pop out of her head, and whenever she visits us she talks baby-talk to me and kisses me right on the mouth, which I despise more than anything else. 'Sweetie pie' she calls my mother, whom she goes out with in the evening, much to my father's dismay. One time they're going to a masquerade at Folkets Hus and I hold the mirror while they put on their make-up, and I think my mother is fantastically beautiful as 'The Night Queen'. Ester is a 'coachman from the eighteenth century', and her arms stick out of the puff sleeves like heavy clubs. They have to hurry because my father will be arriving soon. My mother stands there in all of the black tulle, which is covered with hundreds of shiny sequins. They fall off as easily as her own frail happiness. Just as they're going out the door, my father comes home from work. He stares my mother in the face and says, 'Ha, you old scarecrow.' She doesn't answer, just slips past him without a word, on Ester's heels. My father knows that I heard him, and he sits down across from me with an uncertain expression in his kind, melancholy eyes. 'What do you want to be when you grow up?' he asks awkwardly. 'The Night Queen,' I say cruelly, because here is that 'Ditlev' who always has to spoil my mother's fun.

10

I've started middle school and with that the world has begun to widen. I was allowed to continue because my parents have figured out I still won't be much more than fourteen when I finish school, and since they're giving Edvin training, I shouldn't be left out. At the same time, I've finally gotten permission to use the public library on Valdemarsgade, which has a section with children's books. My mother thinks that I'll get even stranger from reading books that are written for adults; and my father, who doesn't agree, doesn't say anything since I come under my mother's authority and in crucial matters he doesn't dare go against the world order. So for the first time I set foot in a library, and I'm speechless with confusion at seeing so many books collected in one place. The children's librarian is named Helga Mollerup, and she's known and loved by many children in the neighborhood because whenever there's no heat or light at home, they're allowed to sit in the reading room right up until the library closes at five o'clock in the evening. They do their homework there or leaf through books, and Miss Mollerup throws them out only if they start getting noisy, because it's supposed to be completely quiet, like in a church. She asks me how old I am and finds books she thinks are right for a ten-year-old. She is tall and slim and pretty, with dark, lively eyes. Her hands are big and beautiful and I regard them with a certain respect, because it's said that she can slap harder than any man. She's dressed like my teacher, Miss Klausen, in a rather long, smooth skirt and a blouse with a low white collar at the neck. But, unlike Miss Klausen, she doesn't seem to suffer from an insurmountable aversion to children – on the contrary. I'm placed at a table with a children's book in front of me, the title and author of which I've fortunately forgotten. I read, ' "Father, Diana has had puppies." With these words, a slender young girl fifteen years old came storming into the room, where, in addition to the councilman, there were . . .' etc. Page after page. I don't have it in me to read it. It fills me with sadness and unbearable boredom. I can't understand how language – that delicate and sensitive instrument – can be so terribly mistreated, or how such monstrous sentences can find their way into a book that gets into the library where a clever and attractive woman like Miss Mollerup actually recommends it to defenseless children to read. For now, however, I can't express these thoughts, so I have to be content with saying that the books are boring and that I would rather have something by Zacharias Nielsen or Vilhelm Bergsøe. But Miss Mollerup says that children's books are exciting if you just have patience enough to keep reading until the plot gets going. Only when I stubbornly insist on having access to the shelves with the adult books does she give in, astonished, and offer to get some books for me if I'll tell her which ones, since I can't go in there myself. 'One by Victor Hugo,' I say. 'It's pronounced Ügó,' she says, smiling, and pats me on the head. It doesn't embarrass me that she corrects my pronunciation, but when I come home with *Les Misérables* and my father says approvingly, 'Victor Hugo – yes, he's good!' I say didactically and self-importantly, 'It's pronounced Ügó.' 'I don't give a damn how it's pronounced,' he says calmly. 'All those kinds of names should be said the way they're spelled. Anything else is just showing off.' It's never any use to come home and tell my parents anything people said who don't live on our street. Once when the school dentist requested that I ask my mother to buy me a toothbrush and I was dumb enough to mention it at home, my mother snapped, 'You can tell her that she can darn well buy you a toothbrush herself!' But whenever she has a toothache, she first goes around suffering for about a week, while the whole house echoes with her miserable moaning. Then, out on the landing, she asks the advice of another woman, who recommends that she pour schnapps on a wad of cotton and hold it against the infected tooth, which she spends several more days doing, with no results. Only then does she get all dressed up in her finest and venture out to Vesterbrogade, where our doctor lives. He takes his pincers and pulls out the tooth and then she has peace for a while. A dentist never comes into the picture.

In the middle school the girls are better dressed and less sniveling than in the primary school. None of them has lice or a harelip, either. My father says that now I'll be going to school with children of people who are 'better off', but that that's no reason for me to look down on my own home. That's true enough. The children's fathers are mostly skilled workers, and I make my father into a 'machinist', which I think sounds better than stoker. The richest girl in the class has a father who owns a barbershop on Gasværksvej. Her name is Edith Schnoor and she lisps from sheer self-importance. Our classroom teacher is named Miss Mathiassen, a small, lively woman who seems to enjoy teaching. Together with Miss Klausen, Miss Mollerup, and the principal at the old school (the one who resembled a witch), she gives me the distinct impression that women can only have influence in the working world if they're completely flat-chested. My mother is an exception; otherwise all the housewives at home on my street have enormous busts that they consciously thrust out as they walk. I wonder why that is. Miss Mathiassen is the only female teacher we have. She's discovered that I like poetry, and it doesn't work to play dumb with her. I save that for the subjects that don't interest me – but there are lots of those. I only like Danish and English. Our English teacher is named Damsgaard, and he can be terribly short-tempered. Then he pounds the table and says, 'Upon my word, I'll teach you!' He uses this mild oath so often that before long he's known exclusively as 'Upon my word'. One time he reads aloud a sentence that's supposed to be especially difficult, and he asks me to repeat it. It goes like this: 'In reply to your inquiry I can particularly recommend you the boarding house at eleven Woburn Place. Some of my friends stayed there last winter and spoke highly about it.' He praises my correct pronunciation, and that's the reason I can never forget that idiotic sentence.

All the girls in my class have poetry albums, and after I've nagged my mother long enough, I get one too. It's brown and it says 'Poetry' on the outside in gold letters. I let some of the girls write the usual verses in it, and in between I put in some of my own poems with the date and my name underneath so that posterity will have no doubt that I was a child genius. I hide it in one of the dresser drawers in the bedroom under a stack of towels and dishcloths, where I think it will be relatively safe from profane eyes. But one evening Edvin and I are home alone because my parents are out playing cards with my aunt and uncle. Otherwise Edvin is usually out in the evening, but he's been too tired for that since he started his apprenticeship. It's a bad workplace, he says, and he often begs my father to let him find a different one. When that does no good, he starts shouting and says that he'll run off to sea and leave home and much more. Then my father shouts, too, and then when my mother interferes in the fight and takes Edvin's side, there's an uproar in the living room that almost drowns out the racket downstairs at Rapunzel's. It's Edvin's fault that nearly every evening now all peace in the living room is destroyed, and sometimes I wish that he'd follow through with his threats and leave. Now he sits sulking and withdrawn, leafing through *Social-Demokraten*, while only the ticking clock on the wall breaks the silence. I'm doing my homework, but the silence between us oppresses me. He stares at me with his dark, thoughtful eyes that are suddenly just as melancholy as my father's. Then he says, 'Aren't you going to bed soon, damn it? You can never be alone in this damn house!' 'You can go into the bedroom, you know,' I answer, hurt. 'I bloody well will, too,' he mumbles, grabbing the newspaper and going out. He slams the door hard after him. A little while later, to my surprise and uneasiness, I hear a burst of laughter from in there. What can be so funny? I go inside and stiffen with horror. Edvin is sitting on my mother's bed with my poor album in his hand. He's completely doubled up with laughter. Bright red in the face with shame, I take a step toward him and put out my hand. 'Give me that book,' I say and stamp my foot. 'You have no right to take it!' 'Oh God,' he gasps and doubles up with laughter, 'this is hilarious. You're really full of lies. Listen to this!' Then, interrupted by fits of laughter, he reads:

Do you remember that time we sailed
along the still, clear stream?
The moon was mirrored in the sea.
Everything was like a lovely dream.

Suddenly you lay the oar to rest,
and let the boat go still.
You said nothing, but my dear –
the passion in your gaze did thrill.

You took me in your arms so strong.
Lovingly you kissed me.
Never, never will I forget
that hour spent with thee.

'Oh no! Ha ha ha!' He falls back and keeps on laughing, and
the tears stream from my eyes. 'I hate you,' I yell, stamping
my foot powerlessly. 'I hate you! I wish you'd drown in a marl
pit!' With those last words, I'm just about to rush out the
door, when Edvin's insane laughter takes on a new, disturbing
sound. I turn around in the doorway and look at him lying on
his stomach across my mother's striped comforter with his
face hidden in the crook of one arm. My precious book has
fallen to the floor. He sobs inconsolably and uncontrollably,
and I am horrified. Hesitantly, I approach the bed, but I don't
dare touch him. That's something we've never done. I dry my
own tears with the sleeve of my dress and say, 'I didn't mean
it, Edvin, the part about the marl pit. I . . . I don't even know
what it is.' He keeps sobbing without answering and suddenly turns over and gives me a hopeless look. 'I hate them,
the boss and the assistants,' he says. 'They . . . beat me . . .
all day and I'll never learn to paint cars. I'm just sent out to

get beer for all of them. I hate Father because I can't change workplaces. And when you come home, you can never be alone. There's not one damn corner where you can have anything for yourself.' I look down at my poetry album and say, 'I can't have anything for myself, either, you know – and neither can Father or Mother. They're not even alone when they . . . when they . . .' He looks at me, surprised, and finally stops crying. 'No,' he says sadly. 'Jesus, I've never thought about that.' He gets up, regretting, of course, that his sister has seen him in a moment of weakness. 'Well,' he says in a tough voice, 'it probably all gets better when you move away from home.' I agree with him about that. Then I go out and count the eggs in the pantry. I take two and move the rest around so it looks like there are more of them. 'I'm going to mix us an egg schnapps,' I yell toward the living room and start the preparations. At that moment, I like Edvin much better than in all the years when he was distant and wonderful, handsome and cheerful. It wasn't really human that he never seemed to feel bad about anything.

II

Gerda is going to have a baby and Tin Snout has vanished. Ruth says he had a wife and children, and that I should never have anything to do with a married man. I can't imagine I'll ever have anything to do with an unmarried man either, but I keep that to myself. My mother says I'll be thrown out if I ever come home with a child. Gerda isn't thrown out. She has just stopped working at the factory where she earned twenty-five kroner a week, and she stays home now with her big stomach, singing and humming all day long, so you can hear from far away that she hasn't lost her good spirits by any means. Her golden braid has long since been cut off, and in my heart I don't call her Rapunzel anymore, although, as a matter of fact, the fairytale girl had had twins by the time the blinded prince found her in the desert. It sounds so nice and remote that you can easily miss it, and when I was little, I never thought about how it might happen. Last year the landlady's Olga had a baby by a soldier, who also disappeared without a trace, but she was over eighteen and she later got married to a policeman who didn't worry about who the child's father was. Whenever I see women with a big stomach, I try my best to stare only at their faces, where I vainly search for a sign of transcendent happiness like in Johannes V. Jensen's poem: 'I carry in my swollen breast a sweet and anxious spring.' They don't have the kind of glorious expression in their eyes I myself will have when I'm someday expecting a child, I'm sure of that. I have to find poems in books of prose because my father doesn't approve of me lugging home poetry collections from the library. 'Castles in the air,' he says contemptuously, 'they have nothing to do with reality.' I've never cared for reality and I never write about it. When I'm reading Herman Bang's *Ved vejen*, my father takes the book between two fingers and says with every sign of disgust, 'You may not read anything by *him*. He wasn't normal!' I know it's terrible not to be normal, and I have my own troubles trying to pretend that I am. So it comforts me that Herman Bang wasn't either, and I finish reading the book in the reading room. I cry when I get to the end: 'Under the grave's turf sleeps poor Marianne. Come, girls, weep for poor Marianne.' I want to write poetry like that, that anyone and everyone can understand. My father doesn't want me to read anything by Agnes Henningsen, either, because she's a 'public female' – which he doesn't bother to explain any further. If he saw the book with my poems, he would probably burn it. After Edvin found it and laughed at it, I always keep it with me – in my school bag during the day, and otherwise in my underpants, where the elastic keeps it from falling out. At night it's under my mattress. Edvin said later, by the way, that he actually thought the poems were good, if only they had been written by someone other than me. 'When you know the whole thing is a lie,' he says, 'you just die laughing over it.' I'm pleased by his praise, because the part about it being a lie doesn't bother me. I know that you sometimes have to lie in order to bring out the truth.

We've gotten new neighbors since Ketty and her mother were thrown out. It's an older couple with a daughter named Jytte. She works in a chocolate store, and in the evening she often visits us when my father is working the graveyard shift. Then she and my mother have lots of fun because my mother gets along best with women who are younger than she is. Jytte gladly brings chocolate to Edvin and me, and we eat it happily, even though my father says that it's probably stolen. As a result of Jytte's generosity, something awful happens to me. One day when I come home from school, my mother says, 'Well, wasn't that a good lunch you had with you today?' I blush and stammer and don't know what she's talking about. I always throw my lunch away untouched because it's wrapped in newspaper. The others have wax paper around theirs, which my mother would never in her life give in to. 'Oh yes,' I say miserably, 'it was great.' 'I wonder whether she really steals it,' says my mother talkatively. 'You'd think the owner would keep an eye out for that.' Relieved, I understand then that there was some chocolate in my lunch packet, and I feel very happy, because that's a sign of love. It's so strange that my mother has never discovered when I'm lying. On the other hand, she almost never believes the truth. I think that much of my childhood is spent trying to figure out her personality, and yet she continues to be just as mysterious and disturbing. Practically the worst thing is that she can hold a grudge for days, consistently refusing to speak to you or listen to what you're saying, and you never find out how you've offended her. She's the same way with my father. Once, when she made fun of Edvin for playing with girls, my father said, 'Oh well, girls are a kind of human being, too.' 'Humph . . .' said my mother, pressed her lips tight, and didn't open them again until at least a week had passed. Actually I was on her side, because of course girls and boys shouldn't play together. They can't at school, either, unless they're sister and brother. But a boy wouldn't dare be seen with his little sister either, and whenever it's absolutely necessary for Edvin and me to go down the street together, I have to walk three paces behind him and under no circumstances reveal that I know him. I'm nothing to brag about. My mother doesn't think so either, because when we're going to the commemoration of Folkets Hus, she makes a serious effort to get me to look half-way decent. She singes my stiff, yellow hair with the curling iron, and tells me briskly to curl up my toes so that they'll fit into a pair of shoes we borrowed from Jytte. 'She's pretty enough, damn it,' consoles my father, who is having trouble himself with the collar on his white shirt that was bought for the occasion. Edvin is now so grown up that he's mad at having to go out with his family, so he omits his usual lovable remarks about how I'm so ugly that I'll never get married. It's a very special evening, because after making a speech to the workers, Stauning will personally present a gift to all of Vesterbro's recruiters, and among them is my father. Sunday after Sunday he trudges up and down stairs in our neighborhood to enlist members in the political club, and my mother brings him to despair by withdrawing him from it once a month whenever the membership fee of fifty øre is due. Then he mumbles a bunch of curses, grabs his old hat, and rushes after the man to sign up again. She harbors an inarticulate hatred for Stauning and the party, and now and then she hints that my father was once something almost as criminal as a Communist. She doesn't say the word out loud – she doesn't dare – but sometimes I think about the forbidden book he was always reading during my early childhood, the one with the red flag that the happy worker family is looking up at, so there's probably some truth to her insinuations.

My heart beats faster when Stauning goes up to the podium, and I'm sure that my father's does, too. Stauning speaks the way he usually does, and I understand at most half of it. But I enjoy his calm, dark voice that soothingly settles over my soul, assuring me that nothing really evil can happen to us, as long as Stauning exists. He talks about instituting the eight-hour day, even though that's a long time ago now. He talks about the unions and about the criminal scabs who should never be tolerated at any workplace. I quickly promise myself, Stauning, and our Lord that I will never be a scab. Only when he talks about the Communists, who damage and divide the party, does he raise his voice to an angry thunder, which quickly gives way, however, to a soft, almost gentle explanation of the unemployment, which my mother isn't alone in blaming him for. But no, it's due solely to the worldwide depression, he says, and I find the expression pleasant sounding and appealing. I imagine a deeply grieving world where everyone has pulled down their shades and turned off the lights, while the rain streams down from a gray and inconsolable heaven without a single star. 'And now,' says Stauning finally, 'I have the great pleasure of presenting a prize to each of our industrious recruiters as a reward for their work for our great cause!' I blush with pride that my father is among them and look sideways at where he's sitting. He twists his mustache nervously and smiles at me, as if he knows that I share his joy. The battle over the workplace is still creating a coldness between him and Edvin, who looks as though he's about to fall asleep. Then Stauning says each name loudly and clearly, grasps each man's hand in turn, and gives each a book. Everything swims before my eyes when it's my father's turn. The book he receives is called *Poetry and Tools*, and Stauning has written his name and some words of acknowledgement on the title page. On the way home, my father, who is still elated over the honor, says: 'I'll let you read it when you're grown up. I know you like poetry.' My mother and Edvin aren't with us. They're going to the dance afterwards, which doesn't interest my serious father, and I'm only a child. Later my mother puts the book so far back on the bookshelf that you can't see it when the glass door is closed. 'A lovely reward for wearing out the steps every blessed Sunday,' she says scornfully to my father. 'And then he talks about scabs and being underpaid. Good Lord!' My father isn't allowed to have his happiness in peace, either.

12

Time passed and my childhood grew thin and flat, paperlike. It was tired and threadbare, and in low moments it didn't look like it would last until I was grown up. Other people could see it too. Every time Aunt Agnete visited us, she said, 'Goodness gracious, how you're growing!' 'Yes,' said my mother and looked at me with pity, 'if only she'd fill out a bit.' She was right. I was as flat as a paper doll and clothes hung from my shoulders like from a hanger. My childhood was supposed to last until I was fourteen, but what was I going to do if it gave out beforehand? You never got answers to any of the important questions. Full of envy, I stared at Ruth's childhood, which was firm and smooth and without a single crack. It looked as if it would outlive her, so that someone else might inherit it and wear it out. Ruth herself wasn't aware of it. When the boys on the street yelled at me, 'How's the weather up there, sister?' she sent a series of oaths and curses after them so that they ran off in terror. She knew I was vulnerable and shy and she always defended me. But Ruth wasn't enough for me anymore. Miss Mollerup wasn't either, because she had so many children to look after, and I was only one of them. I always dreamed of finding a person, just one, to whom I could show my poems and who would praise them. I had started thinking a lot about death, and I thought of it as a friend. I told myself that I wanted to die, and once when my mother went into town, I took our bread knife and sawed at my wrist, hoping to find the artery – all the while bawling at the thought of my despairing mother who would soon throw herself sobbing over my corpse. All that happened was that I got some cuts; I still have faint marks from them. My only consolation in this uncertain, trembling world was writing poetry like this:

> Once I was young and all aglow,
> full of laughter and fun.
> I was like a blushing rose.
> Now I am old and forgotten.

I was twelve years old then. Otherwise all of my poems were still 'full of lies', as Edvin said. Most of them dealt with love, and if you were to believe them, I was living a wanton life filled with interesting conquests.

I was convinced that I would be sent to a reformatory if my parents ever saw a poem like this:

> It was joy I felt, my friend,
> when our lips met,
> knowing this was the moment
> we were born for – and yet . . .
>
> My vague young dream vanished.
> The door to life stands open.
> Life is beautiful, my friend, thanks,
> you christened me in passion.

I wrote love poems to the man in the moon, to Ruth, or to no one at all. I thought my poems covered the bare places in my childhood like the fine, new skin under a scab that hasn't yet fallen off completely. Would my adult form be shaped by my poems? I wondered. During that time I was almost always depressed. The wind in the street blew so cold through my tall, thin body that the world regarded with disapproving looks. In school I always sat and glared at the teachers, as I did at all grownup people. One day a substitute music teacher calmly came over to my seat, and said quietly but clearly, 'I don't like your face.' I went home and stared at it in the mirror over the dresser. It was pale, with round cheeks and frightened eyes. Across my top front teeth there were small dents in the enamel, which came from having had rickets as a child. I knew that from the school dentist, who said you got the disease from bad nutrition. I kept that to myself, of course, because it wasn't anything to talk about at home. When I couldn't explain my growing melancholy to myself, I thought that the worldwide depression had finally hit me. I also thought a lot about my early childhood, which would never return, and it seemed to me that everything was better then. In the evening, I sat up on the windowsill and wrote in my poetry album:

> Slender strings that break
> are ne'er tied together again,
> unless their tone does slake,
> unless a note does die then.

Then, unlike later on, there wasn't any Kai Friis Møller to whisper in my ear, 'Watch out for inverted word order, Miss Ditlevsen, and for the word ne'er!' My literary models at that time were hymns, ballads, and the poets of the 90s.

One morning I woke up and felt really terrible. My throat hurt and I was freezing as I stepped out onto the floor. I asked my mother whether I could stay home from school but she frowned and told me to spare her such nonsense. She couldn't stand unexpected events or visits that weren't announced ahead of time. Burning with fever, I went to school and was sent home already during first period. By then my mother had collected herself and accepted that I was sick. I fell asleep as soon as I got into bed again and when I woke up, my mother was in the midst of a massive house-cleaning of the whole apartment. She was hanging up clean curtains in the bedroom, and turned around when I called. 'It's good you woke up,' she said. 'The doctor will be here in a little while; if only I get done.' I was terribly afraid of the welfare doctor, and my mother was, too. When she had changed the bed linens and dug out my ears with a bobbypin, the doorbell rang and, flustered, she rushed out and opened the door. 'Hello,' she said respectfully, 'I apologize for the inconvenience . . .' She didn't get any further before she was interrupted by his violent fit of coughing. Hacking and sputtering into his handkerchief, the doctor swept her aside with his cane. 'Yes, yes,' he bellowed when he caught his breath. 'All those stairs – they'll be the death of me. And there's no room to breathe. It's no way to run a practice. I remember you well – you're the one with the teeth. But who in heaven's name is sick? Oh, it's your daughter – where the hell is she?' 'In here.' My mother led the way and the doctor pulled in his stomach with great difficulty as he went past the marriage bed over to me. 'Well,' he shouted and bent his face over me, 'what's the matter with you? You're not playing hooky, are you?' He looked loathsome, and I pulled the comforter all the way up to my chin. He fixed his bulging black eyes on me and I felt like saying that even though we were poor, we were not in the least deaf. His hands were densely covered with hair and a thick black tuft stuck out of each ear. He roared for a spoon, and my mother just about fell over her own feet as she ran off to the kitchen to get one. He shone a little light down my throat and felt the sides of my neck and then said ominously, 'Is there diphtheria in your school? Well? Any of your classmates?' I nodded. Then he grimaced as if he tasted something sour and shouted, 'She's got diphtheria! She has to go to the hospital at once! God damn it!' My mother stared at me reproachfully, as if she'd never expected me to present a busy doctor with anything so impudent. The doctor grabbed his cane furiously and stomped into the living room to write up an admission form. I was horrified. The hospital! My poems! Where should I hide them now? Sleep overpowered me again, and when I woke up, my mother was sitting on the edge of the bed. She asked very gently if there was anything I wanted, and to please her, I asked for a piece of chocolate even though I knew that I couldn't swallow it. Thanks to Jytte, we always had chocolate in the house now. While we waited for the ambulance, I explained to her that I wanted to take my poetry album with me in case someone at the hospital would like to write in it. She had no objection. She sat next to me in the ambulance and stroked my forehead or my hands the whole time. I couldn't remember when she'd ever done that before, and it made me both embarrassed and glad. Whenever I walked down the street or stood in shops, I always looked with a mixture of joy and envy at mothers who held their small children in their arms or caressed them. Maybe my mother had done that once, but I couldn't remember it. At the hospital, I was put in a big ward where there were children of all ages. We all had diphtheria, and most of them were just as sick as I was. I put my poetry album in a drawer, and no one thought it strange that I had it there. Although I lay there for three months, I remember almost nothing about my stay. During visiting hours, my mother stood outside the window and shouted in to me. Shortly before I went home, she talked to the head doctor, who said that I was anemic and didn't weigh enough. Both things hurt my mother's feelings. During the first days after I came home, she made me rye porridge and other fattening foods, even though my father was unemployed again. During my long absence, Ruth had attached herself to the landlady's fat, white-haired Minna, who would soon be thirteen, and with whom she was now always hanging around the trash-can corner, even though she wasn't nearly old enough for that kind of promotion. I felt abandoned and alone. Only the night and the rain and my silent evening star – and my poetry album – gave me some slight comfort during that time. I wrote poetry exclusively like this:

> Wistful raven-black night,
> kindly you wrap me in darkness,
> so calm and mild, my soul you bless,
> making me drowsy and light.

> The rain quiet and fine
> drums so softly at the window.
> I lay my head on the pillow
> on the cool linen's incline.

> Quietly I sleep,
> blessed night, my best friend.
> Tomorrow I'll wake to life again
> my soul in sorrow deep.

One day my brother said to me that I should try to sell one of my poems to a magazine, but I didn't think anyone would pay money for them. I didn't really care, either, as long as someone would print them, but I would never come face to face with that 'someone'. Someday when I was grown up, my poems would of course be in a real book, but I didn't know how that would come about. My father probably knew, but he had said that a girl can't be a poet, so I wouldn't tell him anything about it. It was enough for me anyway to write the poems; there was no hurry to show them to a world that so far had only laughed and scorned them.

13

Uncle Peter has killed Granny. At least that's what my parents
and Aunt Rosalia say. He and Aunt Agnete picked her up on
Christmas Eve and there was a violent snowstorm. All three
of them waited at least fifteen minutes for the streetcar, and
in spite of his fabulous wealth, it didn't occur to Uncle Peter
to pay for a taxi home. By evening Granny had pneumonia,
and they put her to bed on a sofa made up in the parlor, which
of course is heated every Christmas, 'But you know,' says my
mother, 'how damp it is in a room that's only heated three
days a year.' There Granny lay all through the Christmas
holidays and received visits from all of us, and she was completely convinced that she was going to die. The rest of us
didn't believe it. She lay in a white, high-necked nightgown,
and her slender hands that looked like my mother's constantly crept restlessly over the comforter, as if searching in
vain for something very important. Now that she didn't have
her glasses on, you saw that her nose was long and sharp, her
eyes deep blue and very clear, and her sunken mouth had a
stern, inflexible expression whenever she wasn't smiling. She
talked nonstop about her funeral and the five hundred kroner

that she lost when Landmands Bank scandalously folded. My mother and my aunts laughed heartily and said, 'You'll have a fine funeral, Mama, when it comes time for that.' I think I was the only one who took her seriously. She was seventy-six years old, after all, so it couldn't be much longer, I thought. We agreed on the hymns to be sung: 'Church bell, not for the big cities but for the little town were you cast', and 'If you've put your hand to the Lord's plough, then don't look back'. The latter was not, of course, a funeral hymn, but Granny and I were both so fond of it, and we sang it together so often whenever I visited her. On my part, there was also a little spite involved in the choice. My father hated that hymn more than any other because the line 'If sobs strangle the voice, then think of the golden harvest' was proof, in his opinion, of the church's animosity toward the working class.

I wanted so much to write a hymn for Granny myself, but I couldn't. I'd tried so many times, but they always sounded like one of the old hymns, so sadly I had to give up. On the second day after Christmas, something terrible happened. The three sisters were sitting by Granny's bed and Uncle Peter was in the room, when suddenly the doorbell rang and one of my cousins opened the door to The Hollow Leg who, in an awful state, pushed his way in to the sickbed. Aunt Rosalia threw her hands over her face and burst into tears. The Hollow Leg swung at her and shouted that she damn well better come home now, or he'd break every bone in her body. Uncle Peter stepped forward and grabbed hold of the drunken man, and we children were shooed out of the room. There was a terrible uproar, women's screams, and, in the midst of it all, Granny's calm and authoritative voice, trying to appeal to any possible remaining decent side of his character. Then suddenly there was silence and we later learned that Uncle Peter had thrown him out bodily. He had never been allowed into their house before. It was the same thing at home on our street. Either the men drank – and most of them did – or else they harbored a violent hatred toward those who did. When Granny grew worse and the doctor said that she most likely wouldn't make it through the crisis, I wasn't allowed to visit her anymore. My mother was over there day and night, and came home with red eyes and discouraging news. When Granny died, I wasn't permitted to see her, either, but Edvin was. He said she looked just like when she was alive. But I did go to the funeral. I sat in Sunday church next to my mother and Aunt Rosalia, and already during the sermon, I was gripped by an attack of hysterical laughter. It was so terrible that I held my handkerchief over my nose and mouth, hoping they would think I was crying like the others. Fortunately, tears ran down my cheeks too. I was horrified that I couldn't feel anything at her death. I had really loved Granny, and the hymns that we'd chosen together were sung. Why then couldn't I grieve? Long after the funeral, my comforter was replaced by Granny's – my mother's only inheritance. In the evening when I pulled it up over me, Granny's special smell of clean linen flooded over me, and then I cried for the first time and understood what had happened. Oh, Granny, you'll never hear me sing again. You'll never spread real butter on my bread again, and what you've forgotten to tell me about your life will now never be revealed. Every evening, for a long time, I cried myself to sleep, for the smell continued to cling to the comforter.

14

'God help you if you don't deliver that wringer in a hurry,' says my mother, tossing the heavy machine over to me; I have to jump so it won't land on my toes. She's standing in the laundry room, bending over a steaming tub, and I know that she's half-insane on that one day of the month. But I'm in a terrible situation. She's given me ten øre to pay for renting the machine, and it costs fifteen øre an hour. It went up five øre last time, and then I had to promise to pay the remaining five øre next time. So they were supposed to get twenty øre today, and I had only ten. 'Mother,' I say timidly, 'I can't help it if it's gone up.' She raises her head and pushes the damp hair from her face. 'Get going,' she says threateningly, and I go out of the steaming room and up to the courtyard, where I look up at the gray sky, as if expecting help from it. It's late in the afternoon, and near the trash cans the usual gang is standing with their heads together. I wish I were one of them. I wish I were like Ruth, who is so little that she disappears in the middle of the crowd. 'Hi, Tove,' she yells happily, because she has no sense of having abandoned me. 'Hi,' I say and suddenly feel hope. I go over and signal Ruth to come over to me. Then I explain my errand to her and she says, 'I'll go along – I'll get it delivered all right. Give me the ten øre – it's better than nothing.' Everything is straightforward for Ruth, who never wonders at the grownups' behavior. I don't much, either, when it concerns my mother, whose unpredictable personality I've accepted. Over on Sundevedsgade, I wait on the corner, ready to flee, while Ruth barges into the shop, throws the machine on the counter with the ten øre, and races over to me. We run all the way to Amerikavej and stand there, out of breath, laughing like in the old days when we'd pulled off something daring. 'The bitch yelled after me,' gasps Ruth. "It costs fifteen øre," she shouted, but she couldn't get past the machine fast enough with that fat stomach. Oh God, that was fun.' The clear tears leave streaks on the pretty little face, and I feel happy and grateful. As we go home, Ruth asks me why I don't want to join in at the trash-can corner. 'They're such fun, the big girls,' she says. 'They have such a great time.' If Ruth is old enough to be there, then I certainly am, too. When we reach the courtyard at home again, only Minna and Grete are in the trash-can corner. What Ruth sees in Minna, I don't know. Grete lives in the front building, and she's the daughter of a divorced mother who is a seamstress like my aunt. She's in the seventh grade, and I don't know her very well at all. She has on a knitted blouse that reveals two tiny little bulges in the front, what I'm so sadly lacking. When she laughs you can see that her mouth is crooked. It's almost dark in the corner, and it stinks terribly from the garbage cans. The two big girls are sitting on top of them, and Minna hospitably makes room for Ruth beside her. So I stand there, bolt upright like a milepost, and can't think of anything to say. This is a promotion that I've looked forward to for years, but now I don't know if there's much to it. 'Gerda is going to have her baby soon,' says Grete, banging her heels against the trash can. 'It'll be retarded like Pretty Ludvig,' says Minna hopefully. 'That's what happens to children who are conceived during a drunken binge.' 'The hell it does,' says Ruth. 'Most of us would be retarded then.' They always talk like that, and they have something nasty and dirty to say about everyone. I wonder whether they talk about us the same way when my back is turned. Giggling, they talk about drinking and sex and secret, unmentionable liaisons. Grete and Minna won't keep their virginity more than an hour after they're confirmed, they say, and they'll be careful not to have kids before they turn eighteen. I've heard it all before from Ruth, and the conversation in the trash-can corner seems to me deadly dull and boring. It oppresses me and makes me long to be away from the courtyard and the street and the tall buildings. I don't know whether there are other streets, other courtyards, other buildings and people. As yet I've only been out to Vesterbrogade whenever I had to buy three pounds of ordinary potatoes at the grocer's, who always gave me a piece of candy, and who later turned out to be 'The Drilling X'. In the daytime, he quietly minded his little store, and at night he fooled the police by breaking into the city's post offices. It took years to catch him. I'm far away in my thoughts when Ruth suddenly says, 'Tove has a boyfriend!' The two big girls crack up with laughter. 'That's a damn lie,' says Minna, 'she's too holy for that!' 'I'll be damned if it's a lie,' maintains Ruth, giving me a big smile, completely without malice. 'I know who it is, too. It's Curly Charles!' 'Oh, ha ha!' They double over with laughter, and I laugh the loudest. I do it because Ruth just wanted to amuse us, but I don't think there's anything funny about it. Gerda goes across the courtyard, sway-backed and weighted down, and the laughter ceases. In her hand she has a net bag with beer bottles that clink against each other. Her short hair has gotten darker than before and she has brown spots on her face. I quickly wish that she'll have a beautiful little baby with a normal mind. A girl, I wish for her, with golden hair in a long thick braid down her back. Maybe Gerda was in love with Tin Snout, for no one can see into a woman's heart. Maybe she cries herself to sleep every night, no matter how much she sings and laughs during the day. Once she stood in the trash-can corner and shouted about what would happen when she turned fourteen. I don't want to follow tradition in that way. I don't want to do it before I meet a man that I love; but no man or boy has looked in my direction yet. I don't want to have a 'stable skilled worker who comes right home with his weekly paycheck and doesn't drink'. I'd rather be an old maid, which I guess my parents have also gradually resigned themselves to. My father is always talking about 'a steady job with a pension' when I've finished school, but that seems to me just as horrible as the skilled worker. Whenever I think about the future, I run up against a wall everywhere, and that's why I want to prolong my childhood so badly. I can't see any way out of it, and when my mother calls me from up in the window, I leave the precious trash-can corner with relief and go upstairs. 'Well,' she says, very kindly, 'did you get the wringer delivered?' 'Yes,' I say, and she smiles at me as if I've successfully completed a difficult task she had given me.

15

Miss Mathiassen has told me to ask at home for permission to go to high school, in spite of the fact that at the exams I couldn't say how long the Thirty Years' War lasted. I'll never learn to understand those kinds of jokes. Miss Mathiassen says I'm intelligent and ought to continue studying. That's what I'd like to do, too, but I know that we can't afford it. Without much hope, I ask my father anyway and he gets strangely agitated and talks contemptuously about bluestockings and female graduates who are both ugly and stuck-up. Once he was going to help me write a composition about Florence Nightingale, but all that he could say about her was that she had big feet and bad breath – so I consulted Miss Mollerup instead. Otherwise my father has written a lot of my papers and gotten good grades from Miss Mathiassen. It didn't misfire until he wrote an essay on America and ended it like this: 'America has been called the land of freedom. Earlier it meant freedom to be yourself, to work, and to own land. Now it practically means freedom to starve to death if you don't have money to buy food.' 'What in the world,' said my classroom teacher, 'do you mean by that nonsense?' I couldn't explain it, and we only got a 'B' for the effort. No, I can't continue my studies, and I can only remain a child for a short time yet. I have to finish school and be confirmed and get a job somewhere in a house where there's a lot to be done. The future is a monstrous, powerful colossus that will soon fall on me and crush me. My tattered childhood flaps around me, and no sooner have I patched one hole than another breaks through somewhere else. It makes me vulnerable and irritable. I talk back to my mother and she says, gloating, 'All right, all right, just wait until you get out among strangers . . .' Their great sorrow is Edvin, who I've gotten so close to since he clashed with our parents. I don't have any deep or painful feelings about him, so he can confide in me whatever he likes without fear. But my father has always believed that he would be something great, because he had so many talents as a child. He could sing and play guitar and he was always the prince in the school play. All the girls in school and in the courtyard had a crush on him, and since we went to the same school, the teachers always said to me with amazement, 'Are you the one who has such a smart, handsome brother?' It pleased my father, too, that he was a member of the working-class Danish Youth group and put body and soul into the party. My father always said that he didn't respect government ministers who had never had a shovel in their hands, so who knows what future he once envisioned for Edvin? Now all of these dreams are crushed. Edvin is just waiting for the golden day when he becomes a journeyman and can bully the poor apprentices himself. He's also waiting to turn eighteen, because then he's going to move away from home and rent a room where he can have his things in peace. He wants to live somewhere where he can have girls visit him, because on that point my mother is completely intransigent. In her eyes, all young girls are enemy agents who are only out to get married and be supported by a skilled worker, whose training his parents have scrimped and saved to pay for. 'And now when he's going to be earning money,' she says bitterly to my father, 'and could pay some of it back, he runs away from home, of course. It's some girl who's put that into his head.' She says things like that when they've come to bed and think I'm asleep. I understand Edvin completely because this isn't a home you can stay in, and when I turn eighteen, I'm going to move out, too. But I also understand that my father is disappointed. Recently, when he and Edvin were fighting, Edvin said that Stauning drank and had mistresses. My father turned bright red in the face with anger and gave him a terrible slap, so that he tumbled over onto the floor. I'd never seen my father hit Edvin before, and he's never hit me, either. One evening when my parents were lying in bed discussing the problem, my father said that they should give Edvin permission to invite his girlfriend home. 'He doesn't have one – no one steady,' said my mother curtly. 'Yes he does,' said my father, 'otherwise he wouldn't be out every evening. You're chasing him away from home yourself this way.' As always, when my father on a rare occasion insisted on something, my mother had to give in, and Edvin was asked to invite Solvejg to coffee the next evening. I know a lot about Solvejg, but I've never met her. I know that she and my brother love each other, and that they're going to get married when he becomes a journeyman. I also know that he visits her home and that her parents like him very much. He met her at a dance at Folkets Hus. She lives on Enghavevej and is seventeen just like him. Her father repairs bicycles and has a workshop on Vesterbrogade. She herself is a trained beautician and earns a lot of money.

The evening arrived and we all watched anxiously over

my mother's movements. I helped her place our only white tablecloth on the table, and Edvin tried in vain to catch her eye in order to smile at her. He had on his confirmation suit that was too short at the wrists and ankles. My father had on his Sunday best and was sitting on the edge of the sofa, fumbling nervously with the knot in his tie, as if he were the guest. I got the platter with the cream puffs and placed it in the middle of the tablecloth. Then the doorbell rang and my brother almost fell over his own feet as he ran out to open the door. Bright laughter sounded from out in the hallway, and my mother pressed her lips tightly together and grabbed her knitting, which she started working on furiously. 'Hello,' she said shortly and gave her hand to Solvejg without looking up. 'Please sit down.' She could just as well have said, 'Go to hell', but it didn't look like Solvejg was aware of the tense atmosphere. She sat down, smiling, and I thought she was very pretty. Her blond hair was in a wreath on her head, she had pink cheeks with deep dimples, and her dark blue eyes had an expression like they were always laughing. She didn't notice how silent we were, but she talked in a cheerful and self-confident manner, as if she were used to giving orders. She talked about her work, about her parents, about Edvin, and about how happy she was to visit him at home. My mother looked more and more unyielding, and knitted as if she were doing piecework. Finally Solvejg noticed it after all, because she said, 'It's really so strange! Since Edvin and I are going to get married, you'll be my mother-in-law, you know.' She laughed heartily over this, but completely alone, and suddenly my mother burst into tears. It was excruciatingly embarrassing, and none of us knew what to do. She cried as she continued to knit, and there was nothing moving or touching about her tears. 'Alfrida!' said my father admonishingly; he never called her by her first name. I desperately grabbed the coffee pot. 'Won't you have another cup?' I asked Solvejg, and poured her a full cup without waiting for an answer. I thought that maybe she might think this was something quite normal for us. 'Thank you,' she said and smiled at me. For a minute everyone was silent. My brother looked down at the tablecloth with a dark expression. Solvejg made much of putting cream and sugar in her coffee. Tears slid like rain out of my mother's fiercely downcast eyes, and suddenly Edvin pushed back his chair so it crashed against the buffet. 'Come on, Solvejg,' he said, 'we're going. I knew she'd ruin everything. Stop blubbering, Mother. I'm going to marry Solvejg whether you like it or not. Goodbye.' With Solvejg in hand, he rushed out to the hall without giving her time to say goodbye. The door banged hard after them. Only then did my mother take off her glasses and dry her eyes. 'There, you see,' she said reproachfully to my father, 'what comes from his insisting on being an apprentice? That girl will never let go of such a goldmine!' Wearily he lay down on the sofa again and loosened his tie and opened the top button of his shirt. 'That's not it,' he said without anger, 'but you're driving your children away like this.'

Edvin never brought any girlfriend home again, and later when he got married, we first saw his wife after the wedding. It wasn't Solvejg.

16

My childhood's last spring is cold and windy. It tastes of dust
and smells of painful departures and change. In school everyone is involved with preparations for exams and confirmation,
but I see no meaning in any of it. You don't need a middle
school diploma to clean house or wash dishes for strangers,
and confirmation is the tombstone over a childhood that now
seems to me bright, secure, and happy. Everything during this
time makes a deep, indelible impression on me, and it's as if
I'll remember even completely trivial remarks my whole life.
When I'm out buying confirmation shoes with my mother, she
says, as the sales-clerk listens, 'Yes, these will be the last shoes
we give you.' It opens a terrifying perspective on the future
and I don't know how I'll go about supporting myself. The
shoes are brocade and cost nine kroner. They have high heels
and, partly because I can't walk in them without spraining my
ankles, and partly because – in my mother's opinion – I'll be
as tall as a skyscraper when I wear them, my father chops off a
piece of the heels with an axe. That makes the toes turn up, but
after all, I'll only wear them on that one day, my mother consoles me. On his eighteenth birthday, Edvin moved to a room

on Bagerstræde, and now I sleep on a bed made up on the sofa in the living room, which I perceive as still another unhappy sign that my childhood is over. Here I can't sit in the window-sill because it's full of geraniums, and there's only a view of the square with the green gypsy wagon and the gas pump with the big round lamp, which once made me exclaim, 'Mother, the moon has fallen down.' I don't remember it myself, and in general the grownups have completely different memories about you than you yourself have. I've known that for a long time. Edvin's memories are different than mine, too, and whenever I ask him whether he can remember some event or other I thought we experienced together, he always says no. My brother and I are fond of each other, but we can't talk to each other very well. When I visit him at his room, his land-lady opens the door. She has a black mustache and seems to suffer from the same suspicions as my mother. 'His sister,' she says, 'that's a good one. I've never known a lodger who has so many sisters and cousins as he has.' Things are not good with Edvin even though he now has a whole room to him-self. He smokes cigarettes and drinks beer and often goes out to dances in the evening with a friend named Thorvald. They were apprentices together and want to have their own work-shop someday. I've never met Thorvald, because neither of us can bring anyone home, no matter what sex they are. Edvin is unhappy because Solvejg has left him. One day she came up to his room where they could finally be alone together, and said that she didn't want to marry him after all. Edvin blames my mother, but I think Solvejg has found someone else. I've read somewhere, you see, that real love only grows greater with opposition, but I keep quiet about that because it's prob-ably better for Edvin to believe that my mother has scared her away. His room is very small and the furniture looks like it's ready for the dump. I never stay very long at Edvin's because there are long pauses between our words, and he looks just as relieved when I leave as he looks happy when I arrive. I talk about little things from home. For example, I wear a pair of oiled leather boots that, as usual, I've inherited from him. My father varnished the soles of them so that they'll last longer and he also gave the toes a couple of swipes, so that they turned up and are completely black while the rest of the boots are brown. One day my mother threw some rags over to me, 'Rub your boots with them and then throw them into the stove,' she said. 'My boots?' I asked happily, and she laughed long and hard at me. 'No, you goof, the rags!' she said. Things like that make Edvin laugh too, and that's why I tell him about it now, when he's no longer part of our daily life. Nothing is like it was before. Only Istedgade is the same, and now I'm allowed to go there in the evening, too. I go there with Ruth and Minna, and Ruth doesn't seem to notice that there is something like hatred between Minna and me. Sometimes we go over to Saxogade to visit Olga, Minna's big sister who married a policeman and has it made. Olga minds the baby and I'm allowed to hold it in my arms. It feels unbelievably nice. Minna wants to marry a man in uniform too, 'because they're so handsome', she says. Then they'll live near Hedebygade, because that's what everyone does when they get married. Ruth nods approvingly and prepares herself for the same fate, which seems desirable to both of them. I smile in agreement as if I'm also looking forward to such a future, and as usual, I'm afraid of being found out. I feel like I'm a foreigner in this world and I can't talk to anyone about the overwhelming problems that fill me at the thought of the future.

Gerda has had a lovely little boy, and she strolls proudly up and down the street with him while her parents are at work.

She's only seventeen, and you're first supposed to have children when you're eighteen. She's disliked because she won't admit by her attitude and bearing that things have gone awry for her and consequently politely accept the pity that the street offers her. Everyone is outraged that she refused to accept the basket full of baby clothes that Olga's mother had collected for her. There she goes, just like that, allowing her parents to support her beyond a reasonable age. 'If that were you,' says my mother, 'you'd have been kicked out long ago.' Oh, how I'd like to hold my own little baby in my arms! I would support it and figure out everything some way or other. If only I'd gotten that far. At night when I'm in bed, I imagine meeting an attractive and friendly young man whom I ask with polite phrases to do me a great favor. I explain to him that I'd very much like to have a child and ask him to see that I get one. He agrees, and I clench my teeth and close my eyes and pretend that it's someone else this is happening to, someone who's of no concern to me. Afterwards, I don't want to ever see him again. But such a young man is not to be found in the courtyard or on our street, and I write a poem in my poetry album, which now lies in the bottom of the buffet drawer:

> A little butterfly flew
> high in the blue-tinged sky.
> All common sense, morality
> and duties did it defy.
>
> Drunk with the spring day's charm
> with trembling wings unfurled,
> it was borne by the sungold rays
> down to the beautiful world.

Tove Ditlevsen

And into a pale pink apple blossom
which had just opened wide,
flew the little butterfly
and found a lovely bride.

And the apple blossom closed,
over was the wild flight.
Oh, thank you, little ones. You've taught me
how to love with delight.

17

My granny was hardly cold in her grave before my father took us out of the state church. The expression was my mother's. Granny doesn't have a grave. Her ashes are in an urn at Bispe-bjerg Crematorium, and I feel nothing standing there looking at that stupid vase. But I go there often because my mother wants me to. She cries steadily every time we're there, and I have a guilty conscience when she says, 'Why aren't you crying? You did at the funeral.' Now that Edvin's gone, I'm always with my mother whenever I'm not in school or down on the street. I've also been to a dance at Folkets Hus with her, but it wasn't fun dancing with her because I'm a head taller than she is and I feel very big and clumsy compared to her. While she was dancing with a gentleman, a young man came and asked me to dance. That had never happened before, and I was about to say no, because I don't know any dance steps other than those my mother taught me at home in the living room when she was in one of her light-hearted moods. But the young man already had his arm around my waist and since he danced well, so did I. He was completely silent, and just to say something, I asked him what he did.

'I'm in the courier corps,' he said briefly. I thought it had something to do with 'curing' and decided he was a doctor. That was certainly something different from a 'stable skilled worker'. Maybe he would dance with me the whole evening, and maybe he was already falling a little in love with me. My heart beat faster and I leaned against him just a little. 'It's night, now the thieves are at work,' he sang in my ear with the music. Suddenly it stopped and he set me next to my mother, bowed stiffly, and disappeared forever. 'He was good-looking,' said my mother. 'If only he comes back.' 'He's a doctor,' I bragged and told her that he was in the courier corps. 'Oh, good God,' laughed my mother, 'that's just a messenger service!'

We're not members of the state church, and for that reason I'm going to have a civil confirmation. That separates me from all the girls in my class who go to a pastor, but it doesn't matter much since I've given up on being like them. They take turns visiting each other on Saturdays when Victor Cornelius plays for the radio's Saturday dances. Boys are invited then too and many of my classmates already have someone they're going steady with. We don't have a radio at home, and it's no fun anymore to put on the headphones and listen to the crackling of the crystal set my brother made at school. And even if we had a radio, my parents wouldn't have been inclined to give a Saturday dance in my honor. I'm taking exams now and I don't care whether I get good or bad grades. Maybe I'm disappointed after all that I can't go to high school. Only one of the girls in my class is allowed to. Her name is Inger Nørgård and she's just as tall and lanky as I am. She never does anything except study and gets A's in every subject. The others say that she'll be an old maid – that's why she's going to continue in school. I've never really talked to her, no more than with anyone else in school. I have to keep everything to myself, and sometimes I think I'm about to suffocate. I've stopped going around on Istedgade in the evening with Ruth and Minna because more and more their conversations consist of nothing but giggling references and coarse, obscene things that can't always be transformed into gentle, rhythmic lines in my increasingly sensitive soul. I only talk to my mother about very trivial things, about what we eat, or about the people who live downstairs. My father has grown very quiet since Edvin moved away, and for him I'm just someone who should 'make a good start', with all the terrible events he imagines with that expression. One day when I'm visiting my brother, he says to my astonishment that his friend Thorvald would like to meet me. He's told Thorvald that I write poems, and he asks if Thorvald may read them. Horrified, I say no, but then my brother says that Thorvald knows an editor at *Social-Demokraten* who might possibly print my poems if they're good. He says this in between fits of coughing because he can't tolerate the cellulose lacquer he works with. Finally I give in and promise to come over with my poetry book the next evening, then Thorvald will look at my poems. Thorvald is also a journeyman painter, eighteen years old, and not engaged. The latter I verify since I've already started dreaming about him as the kind young man who, almost without a word, will understand everything.

With my poetry album in my school bag, I walk over to Bagerstræde the next evening. I look firmly at the people I meet because soon I'll be famous, and then they'll be proud that they met me on my way to the stars. I'm terribly afraid that Thorvald will laugh at my poetry as Edvin did long ago. I imagine that he looks like my brother, except he has a thin black mustache. When I enter Edvin's room, Thorvald is sitting on the bed next to my brother. He stands up and puts out his hand. He is little and solid. His hair is blond and coarse and his face is covered with pimples in all states of ripeness. He is visibly shy and the whole time he runs his hand through his hair so that it stands straight up in the air. I stare at him horrified because I think that I can't possibly show him my poems. 'This is my sister,' says Edvin completely superfluously. 'She's damn pretty,' says Thorvald, twisting his hair in his fingers. I think it's very kind of him to say that, and I smile at him as I sit down on the room's only chair. You shouldn't be swayed by people's appearance, I think, and maybe he really thinks I'm pretty. At any rate, he's the first person who's ever said that. I take the book out of my bag and hold it in my hands for a while. I'm so afraid that this influential person will think the poems are bad. I don't know whether they're any good at all. 'Give it to him now,' says my brother impatiently, and I hand it to him reluctantly. As he pages through it and reads with a serious, furrowed brow, I feel as if I'm in a completely different state of existence. I'm excited and moved and scared and it's as if the book is a trembling, living part of myself that can be destroyed with a single harsh or insulting word. Thorvald reads in silence and there's not a smile on his face. Finally he shuts the book, gives me an admiring look with his pale blue eyes and says emphatically, 'They're damn good!' Thorvald's language reminds me of Ruth's. She can hardly form a sentence, either, without embellishing it with some seldom-varying swear word. But you shouldn't judge a person by that, and at the moment I think Thorvald looks both wise and handsome. 'Do you really think so?' I ask happily. 'God damn, yes,' he avows. 'You can easily sell them.' His father is a printer, Edvin explains, and he knows all the editors. 'Yes,' says Thorvald with pride, 'I'll take care of it, by

God. Just let me take the book home and I'll show it to the old man.' 'No,' I say quickly, and grab for the book. 'I . . . I want to go there myself and show it to this editor. You just need to tell me where he lives.' 'All right,' says Thorvald amenably. 'I'll tell Edvin and then he can explain it to you.' I pack the book away in my school bag again and am in a hurry to get home. I want to be alone to dream about my happiness. Now it doesn't matter about confirmation, it doesn't matter about growing up and going out among strangers, it doesn't matter about anything except the wonderful prospect of having just one poem printed in the newspaper.

Thorvald and Edvin keep their word, and a couple of days later I have a note in my hand on which it says: 'Editor Brochmann, Sunday Magazine, *Social-Demokraten*, Nørre Farimagsgade 49, Tuesday, two o'clock.' I put on my Sunday clothes, rub my mother's pink tissue paper across my cheeks, make her think that I'm going to take care of Olga's baby, and stroll out to Nørre Farimagsgade. I find the door in the big building with the editor's name on a sign and knock cautiously. 'Come in,' sounds from the other side. I step into an office where an old man with a white beard is sitting at a big, cluttered desk. 'Sit down,' he says very kindly and motions toward a chair. I sit down and am gripped by an intense shyness. 'Well,' he says, taking off his glasses, 'what do you want?' Since I'm unable to utter a word, I can't think of what else to do except hand him the by now rather grubby little book. 'What's this?' He leafs through it and reads a couple of the poems half-aloud. Then he looks at me over his glasses: 'They're very sensual, aren't they?' he says, astonished. I turn bright red in the face and say quickly, 'Not all of them.' He reads on and then says: 'No, but the sensual ones are the best, by God. How old are you?' 'Fourteen,' I say. 'Hmm . . .' Irresolutely he strokes his beard. 'I only edit the children's page, you know, and we can't use these. Come back in a couple of years.' He snaps shut my poor book and hands it to me, smiling. 'Goodbye, my dear,' he says. Somehow or other I edge myself out the door with all my crushed hopes. Slowly, numbed, I walk through the city's spring, the others' spring, the others' joyous transformation, the others' happiness. I'll never be famous, my poems are worthless. I'll marry a stable skilled worker who doesn't drink, or get a steady job with a pension. After that deadly disappointment, a long time passes before I write in my poetry album again. Even though no one else cares for my poems, I have to write them because it dulls the sorrow and longing in my heart.

18

During the preparations for my confirmation, the big question is whether The Hollow Leg will be invited. He has never visited us before, but now all of a sudden he's stopped drinking. He sits the whole day drinking just as many bottles of soda pop as he used to drink beers. My mother and father say it's a great joy for Aunt Rosalia. But she doesn't look happy, because the man is completely yellow in the face from a bad liver and apparently doesn't have long to live. The family thinks that's to her advantage, too. Now I'm allowed to visit them and it's no longer necessary to protect me from seeing and hearing anything that's not good for me. But Uncle Carl hasn't changed at all. He still mumbles gruffly and inarticulately down at the table about the rotten society and the incompetent government ministers. At intervals he issues short, telegraphic orders to Aunt Rosalia, who obeys his slightest gesture as she always has. The soda pop bottles are lined up in front of him and it's incomprehensible that any person is capable of consuming so much liquid. I wonder at my parents. When you go down into the basement for coal, you usually fall over some drunk who's sleeping it off wrapped up in the ruins of an overcoat, and on the street, drunken men are such an everyday sight that no one bothers to turn around to look at them. Almost every evening, a bunch of men stand in the doorway drinking beer and schnapps, and it's only the very young children who are afraid of them. But throughout our whole childhood, we weren't allowed to see Uncle Carl, even though it would have pleased Aunt Rosalia beyond words. After long discussions between my mother and father and between my mother and Aunt Agnete, it's decided that he will be invited to my confirmation. So the whole family will be there except for my four cousins, since there's just not room for them in the living room. My mother is in a good mood because of the big event, and she says I'm ungrateful and odd because I can't hide that I think all of the preparations have nothing to do with me.

The exams are over and we've had the graduation party at school. Everyone cheered now that they were leaving the 'red prison', and I cheered loudest of all. It bothers me a lot that I don't seem to own any real feelings anymore, but always have to pretend that I do by copying other people's reactions. It's as if I'm only moved by things that come to me indirectly. I can cry when I see a picture in the newspaper of an unfortunate family that's been evicted, but when I see the same ordinary sight in reality, it doesn't touch me. I'm moved by poetry and lyrical prose, now as always – but the things that are described leave me completely cold. I don't think very much of reality. When I said goodbye to Miss Mathiassen, she asked me whether I'd found a position. I said yes, and chattered on with false cheerfulness about how I was going to home economics school in a year and until then I had an au pair job at a woman's home where I would take care of her child. All of the others were going to work in offices or stores and I was ashamed that I was only going to be a mother's helper. Miss Mathiassen looked at me searchingly with her wise, kind eyes. 'Well, well,' she sighed, 'it's a shame though that you couldn't go to high school.' As soon as my confirmation is over, I'm going to start my job. I went there with my mother to apply for it. The woman was divorced and treated us with cool condescension. She didn't look as if she would be interested in discovering I wrote poetry and just had to pass the time until I could go back to Editor Brochmann at *Social-Demokraten* in a couple of years. It wasn't very elegant in the apartment, either, even though there was of course a grand piano and carpets on the floor. She's at work during the day and in the meantime I'm supposed to clean, cook, and take care of the boy. I haven't done any of these things before, and I don't know how I'm going to be worth the twenty-five kroner I'm supposed to earn every month. Behind me is my childhood and school, and before me an unknown and dreaded life among strangers. I'm closed in and caught between these two poles, the way my feet are squeezed down into the long, pointed brocade shoes. I sit in the Odd Fellows Hall between my parents and listen to a speech about youth as the future all of Denmark is counting on, and about how we must never disappoint our parents who have done so much for us. All of the girls are sitting with a bouquet of carnations in their laps just like me, and they look as though they're just as bored. My father is tugging at his stiff collar and Edvin is suffering from fits of coughing. The doctor said he should change jobs, but that's impossible, of course, after he's been through four years of training to become a journeyman painter. My mother is wearing a new black silk dress with three cloth roses at the neck, and her newly permed hair frizzes around her head. She had to fight to have it done, partly because my father didn't think they could afford it, and partly because he thinks it's 'new-fangled' and 'loose'. I liked her hair better when it was long and smooth. Now and then she puts her handkerchief up to her eyes, but I don't know whether she's really crying. I can't see any reason for it. I think about the fact that once the most important thing in the world was whether my mother liked me; but the child who yearned so deeply for that love and always had to search for any sign of it doesn't exist anymore. Now I think that my mother cares for me, but it doesn't make me happy.

We have pork roast and lemon mousse for dinner, and my mother, who gets angry and irritable at any domestic effort, doesn't relax until it's time for dessert. Uncle Carl is seated next to the stove and he sweats so much he has to constantly wipe his bald, round head with his handkerchief. At the other end of the table sits Uncle Peter, who is a carpenter and represents the cultured branch of the family along with Aunt Agnete, who sang in the church choir as a child. She has written a song for me because she has a 'vein' that flows on all such occasions. It deals with various uninteresting events of my childhood and each verse ends like this: 'God be with you on your way, fa-la-la, then luck and happiness will always follow you, fa-la-la.' When we sing the refrain, Edvin looks at me with laughter in his eyes, and I hurriedly look at the printed words of the song in order not to smile. Then Uncle Peter taps his glass and stands up. He's going to make a speech. It's like the one at the Odd Fellows Hall, and I only listen with half an ear. It's something about stepping into the adult ranks and being hard-working and clever like my parents. It's a little too long. Uncle Carl says, 'Hear, hear!' every second, as if he'd been drinking wine, and Edvin coughs. My mother has shining eyes and I cringe with discomfort and boredom. When he's done and everyone has said 'Hurrah', Aunt Rosalia says softly as she envelops me with her warm glance, 'The adult ranks – Good Lord! She's neither fish nor fowl.' I can feel my lips quiver and quickly look down at my plate. That's the most loving and maybe also the truest thing that is said at my confirmation. After dinner everyone can finally stretch their legs, and they all seem to be in a better mood than when they arrived, maybe also because of the wine. They admire the little wristwatch that I got from my parents. I like it too, and think that it makes my thin wrist look a little more substantial. I got money from the others, more than fifty kroner, but it's to be put in the bank for my old age, so that doesn't excite me much.

After the guests have left and I've helped my mother clean up, we sit together at the table and talk for a while. Even though it's past midnight, I'm wide awake and very relieved that my party is over. 'God, how he stuffed himself,' says my mother, meaning Uncle Peter. 'Did you see that?' 'Yes,' says my father indignantly, 'and drank! When it's free he can really put it away.' 'And he pretended that Carl wasn't even there,' continues my mother. 'I felt bad for Rosalia.' Suddenly she smiles at me and says, 'Wasn't it a lovely day, Tove?' I think about how much trouble and expense this has cost them. 'Oh yes,' I lie, 'it was a good confirmation.' My mother nods in agreement and yawns. Then she's struck by an idea. 'Ditlev,' she says with a happy voice, 'since Tove is going to be earning money now, can't we afford to buy a radio?' The blood rushes to my head with fright and rage. 'You're not going to buy a radio with my money,' I say hotly. 'I have plenty of use for it myself.' 'I see,' says my mother, cold as ice, getting up and stomping out the door, which she slams after her so that the plaster clatters down from the wall. My father looks at me, embarrassed. 'Don't take it so literally,' he explains. 'We have a little in the bank – we can use that to buy a radio. You just have to pay for your room and board here at home.' 'Yes,' I say, regretting my temper. Now my mother won't speak to me for days, I know. My father says good night kindly and goes into the bedroom, where I'll never again sit on the windowsill and dream about all the happiness that's only attainable by grown-up people.

I'm alone in my childhood's living room where my brother once sat and pounded nails into a board while my mother sang and my father read the forbidden book I haven't seen for years. It's all centuries ago and I think that I was very happy then, in spite of my painful feeling of childhood's end-lessness. On the wall hangs the sailor's wife staring out to sea. Stauning's serious face looks down at me, and it's a long time since my God was created in his image. Although I'm going to be sleeping at home, I feel like I'm saying goodbye to the room tonight. I have no desire to go to bed, and I'm not sleepy, either. I'm seized by a vast sadness. I move the gera-niums on the windowsill and look up at the sky where an infant star shines in the bottom of the new moon's cradle, which rocks gently and quietly between the shifting clouds. I repeat to myself some lines from Johannes V. Jensen's *Bræen*, which I've read so often that I know long passages by heart. 'And now like the evening star, then like the morning star shines the little girl who was killed at her mother's breast; white and self-absorbed like a child's soul that wanders alone and plays so well by itself on endless roads.' Tears run down my cheeks because the words always make me think of Ruth, whom I've lost for good. Ruth with the fine, heart-shaped mouth and the strong, clear eyes. My little lost friend with the sharp tongue and the loving heart. Our friendship is over just as my childhood is. Now the last remnants fall away from me like flakes of sun-scorched skin, and beneath looms an awkward, an impossible adult. I read in my poetry album while the night wanders past the window – and, unawares, my childhood falls silently to the bottom of my memory, that library of the soul from which I will draw knowledge and experience for the rest of my life.